PENGUIN BOOKS

DON CAMILLO AND T

Giovanni Guareschi lived at Parma, near the River Po, where he was born in 1908. As he himself recounted, his parents wished him to be a naval engineer: consequently he studied law, made a name as a sign-board painter, and among other jobs, gave mandolin lessons. His father had a heavy black moustache under his nose: Giovanni grew one just like it. He always wore it and was proud of it. He was not bald, wrote eight books, and was five feet ten inches tall. 'I also have a brother,' Guareschi said, adding, 'but I prefer not to discuss him. And I have a motor-cycle with four cylinders, an automobile with six cylinders, and a wife and two children.'

As a young man he drew cartoons for *Bartoldo*. When the war came he was arrested by the political police for howling in the streets all one night. In 1943 he was captured by the Germans at Alessandria and adopted the slogan: 'I will not die even if they kill me.' Back in Italy after the war he became editor-in-chief of *Candido* at Milan. He scripted a film, *People Like This*.

Giovanni Guareschi died in 1968.

GIOVANNI GUARESCHI

Don Camillo
and the Devil

PENGUIN BOOKS

Penguin Books Ltd, Harmondsworth, Middlesex, England
Penguin Books Inc., 7110 Ambassador Road,
Baltimore, Maryland 21207, U.S.A.
Penguin Books Australia Ltd, Ringwood, Victoria, Australia
Penguin Books Canada Ltd,
41 Steelcase Road West, Markham, Ontario, Canada
Penguin Books (N.Z.) Ltd,
182–190 Wairau Road, Auckland 10, New Zealand

First published in Great Britain by Gollancz 1957
Published in Penguin Books 1962
Reprinted 1964, 1966, 1968, 1974, 1976

Copyright © the Estate of Giovanni Guareschi, 1957

Made and printed in Great Britain
by Richard Clay (The Chaucer Press) Ltd
Bungay, Suffolk
Set in Monotype Baskerville

Contents

Operation Saint Babila

SAINT BABILA was perpetually in Don Camillo's way, but Don Camillo didn't know how in the world to get rid of him. On that far-away day when he first came to take over the parish he found Saint Babila in the sacristy, and there he left him. Every now and then he moved him from one corner to another, but Saint Babila continued to be cumbersome, because he was in the form of a life-size terracotta statue, six feet tall and heavy as lead.

In the beginning the statue must have been properly robed and vested, with artistically painted face and hands, but the passage of time had caused all the ornamentation to fall to pieces, leaving the terracotta crude and bare. If it hadn't been for the worn inscription 'Saint Babila, B–' (for Bishop) on the base, no one would have thought there was anything holy about it. Several generations of acolytes had chosen to use it as a coat-rack, and as a result the head and shoulders looked as if they had been thoroughly sandpapered. From the waist down it might have been modelled with a shovel, and from the waist up brushed with a chicken feather.

For years, then, Saint Babila had been a nuisance to Don Camillo. Any number of times he had thought of getting rid of him, but even though it is made of identical material, a saint's statue is not the same thing as a chipped kitchen pot. You can't take a hammer and smash it, or simply toss it into the dustbin. And even if banished to the cellar or woodshed it remains just as cumbersome as before. Don Camillo had in mind at one point to haul it all the way to the barn, but he was afraid that the loft floor would collapse under its weight. If only it had been made out of bronze, he could have melted it down and recast it as a bell. But how can a sacred image, sculptured in terracotta, be destroyed without profanity? One day, however, Don Camillo did find the answer, and he hurried at once to the sacristy to talk it over with Saint Babila.

The saint stood in one corner, his worn head and shoulders emerging from a crude vestment whose folds, moulded by some rustic potter, made it look as if it were a piece of corrugated sheet-iron.

'I have it!' said Don Camillo. 'And it's for your good as well as mine.' Then, removing the incense-pot censer which an irreverent acolyte had hung round the saint's neck, he continued:

'This is no place for you. Here there's no telling who may lay dirty hands upon you and fail to show the respect that is your due. I'm going to take you to a refuge where no one can touch you and you can abide in safety for ever and for ever. No, I'm not going to bury you underground, either. Underground means death, and running water is life-giving. . . .'

Don Camillo fancied he detected a grimace on the saint's worn face, and he protested impatiently:

'What about the "Christ of the Deep Sea" near Portofino? Wasn't his statue purposely lowered into the ocean bottom? You've no reason to make trouble! . . .'

Saint Babila made no trouble, and that very night Don Camillo proceeded to carry out his plan. It required an immense physical effort, because the statue weighed over three hundred pounds. Finally, however, without being seen by a single soul, he succeeded in removing it from the sacristy and loading it on to a wagon. A few minutes later, with his overcoat pulled up to his hat-brim, he got into the driver's seat and drove towards the river. The night seemed particularly propitious to an Operation Saint Babila. It was freezing cold and the countryside was deserted.

When they reached the river, Don Camillo persuaded the horse to go all the way down to the water's edge, where with the help of two long boards he pushed the statue on to a rowing-boat. Then, having loosened the rope by which the boat was tied up, he took the oar and rowed towards midstream. He had a very clear idea of where he was going. The river, at this point, was so wide that it seemed like the sea and had a particularly deep bottom. This was to be the resting-place of Saint Babila.

At the last minute the saint abandoned his docile behaviour and made so much trouble that Don Camillo nearly fell overboard. But eventually the statue resigned itself to making the plunge and disappeared into the river.

When he got back home Don Camillo put the horse in the stable and before going to bed went to pay his respects to the Christ over the main altar.

'Lord,' he said, 'thank you for not letting Saint Babila drag me into the water. I have reason to be happy to-night, because Saint Babila is settled *per omnia saecula saeculorum*, and that means for ever and ever.'

'*Amen*,' murmured Christ with a smile. 'But remember, Don Camillo, that in human events there are no absolutes.'

Operation Saint Babila had taken place between eleven-thirty and one-forty-five of a freezing November night, without a single soul to see. Don Camillo had conducted it with extreme prudence and had no cause for worry. But since in human events there are no absolutes, it happened that at one-forty-seven of the same night Comrade Peppone, the Communist mayor of the village, was awakened by a pole knocking against the shutters of his bedroom window. He got up and cautiously opened the shutters, to find that one of his Party henchmen, Smilzo, was standing below, at the far end of the pole, trembling with cold and excitement.

'Chief,' he shouted, 'something very serious has happened.'

Peppone went downstairs to open the door. As soon as Smilzo was in the house he exclaimed:

'A sacrilege!'

'A sacrilege?' echoed Peppone. 'Who's guilty of a sacrilege?'

'The priest!' shouted Smilzo.

Peppone took hold of Smilzo's ragged jacket and shook him violently.

'Smilzo, you must have been drinking.'

'Not I, Chief. The priest has committed a sacrilege, I tell you. I saw him with my own eyes and followed him the whole way. Do you remember the dusty statue of Saint Babila that stood in one corner of the sacristy?'

Peppone did remember. 'Saint Babila, B –' (for Blessed Virgin, he imagined), he must have read those words a thousand times on the base of the statue, which had most often been seen serving as a rack for coats and vestments.

'Well, I saw that statue, I tell you. He put it on a wagon and took it down to the river, then he transferred it to a boat and threw it into the water. I didn't see him actually throw it but I heard the splash, and when the boat came back there was no more no statue. That's a sacrilege, Chief!'

This was quite obviously true. Otherwise Don Camillo would not have feared the light of day. If he had done it all alone, in the dead of night, then there must have been something reprehensible about it.

This was the period of 'peaceful co-existence', when the Reds changed their line and passed themselves off as quiet folk, with a genuine respect for other people and especially for other people's religion. Peppone wasted no time. He got dressed and went with Smilzo to check up on what had taken place. Peeping through the sacristy window he saw that the statue had disappeared. Then he found the imprint of the horseshoes and the track left by the wagon-wheels, all leading down to the river. On the shore there was a still more important piece of evidence. While Don Camillo was transferring the statue to the boat, a fragment had been chipped off and now lay there, bearing witness to the truth of Smilzo's story. With all these elements in hand, Peppone sent Smilzo to gather his henchmen together. At eleven o'clock the next morning the village was plastered with posters carrying the following message:

Citizens:

Under cover of darkness a sacrilegious hand profaned the Lord's House and stole the sacred image of the Virgin Saint Babila. In order to abolish its veneration and to uproot even its memory from the hearts of the faithful, this same sacred image was then, most nefariously, thrown into the river.

Before this ignoble deed the local section of the Communist Party cannot but lay aside its political enmity towards the clerical intriguers. Along with all good Christians we deplore this loss and intend to organize a searching party, whose mission is to restore Saint Babila to the place of honour which she held before.

Giuseppe Bottazzi

Everyone that read these words hastened to the church, and since the whole village read them the church was soon overcrowded and Don Camillo was in serious trouble. People wanted to know how, when, and why, and he couldn't very well answer: 'There was no theft and no sacrilege. I am the one that threw the statue into the river.' Suddenly now that the statue was gone, all the villagers, including those who were completely unaware of its existence, declared that it was the church's most treasured possession. Words could not express the resentment they harboured against the thief.

When Don Camillo could stand no more, he threw out his arms in a gesture of despair and fled to the rectory, where he took to his bed with a raging fever.

'Poor Don Camillo!' said his parishioners. 'He's overcome by sorrow.'

Meanwhile the proponents of the 'peaceful co-existence' line had gone into action, and the next morning they were hot on the trail, down by the river. From a motor-boat, where he cut the figure of an admiral, Peppone directed dredging operations. In the area pointed out by Smilzo not a single inch of the river bottom was left untouched. And when the workers came back to the shore for lunch, Peppone announced:

'If we're unsuccessful we'll call upon the union of deep-sea divers. Saint Babila shall be found; we have sworn it before God and the people!'

This fine phrase made the round of the entire village. Meanwhile, after lunch, the dredging was resumed, and soon the search centred about the deepest part of the river. All of a sudden a cry passed from mouth to mouth on the shore:

'They're getting hot!'

And half an hour later there was a loud explosion of joy:

'Saint Babila is found!'

Don Camillo was still nursing his fever and trying to keep his mind off his troubles when they were quite forcibly called to his attention. A crowd of excited men and women burst into his room shouting:

'Father, they've fished up the statue!'

'Father, they're forming a procession on the bank of the river!'

'Father, the procession is on its way, bringing the statue home!'

'The whole village is marching, and a lot more people from the country around!'

'Father, you'll simply have to get up and receive them!'

The procession was indeed drawing near. When Don Camillo sat up in bed and looked out of the window he could see a multitude of people winding their way along and singing: 'Look down on the people, Thou Blessed One', to the music of the local brass band. There was nothing to do but get dressed and go downstairs. He threw open the church door and stood there, waiting for Saint Babila.

They had put the statue on a litter, borne on the shoulders of the eight liveliest devils of Peppone's gang, with Peppone himself and his closest cronies preceding it. Behind the litter came the brass band, followed by some two or three thousand people. Those of the villagers who had stayed at home scattered flowers from their windows.

When the head of the procession reached the church square and the litter-bearers were in front of the door, Peppone signalled to them to lay their burden gently down. The winding line broke up and rushed forward. When the crowd had gathered round him Peppone turned to Don Camillo and said in a thundering voice:

'Father, the people's callous but honest hands have brought you back the venerable image of their protectress, Saint Babila, stolen by some sacrilegious criminal but washed and purified in the waters of our country's mightiest river!'

Don Camillo wished for his eyes to be transformed into loaded machine-guns, but all he could do was bow his head as if to say: 'Thank you, Mr Mayor. May the heavens open and strike you dead!'

After this a group of true believers took the place of Peppone's henchmen and Saint Babila was carried triumphantly into the church. Naturally the statue could not be banished to the sacristy. The image of Saint Lucius, patron of dairy-farmers, was moved out of one of the chapels in order to give it an honoured place.

An hour later, when peace and quiet were restored, the wife of Bigio came to the church to have her latest offspring baptized. The baby was a girl, and if she hadn't been the offspring of a rascally infidel, she might have been called pretty.

'What do you want to call her?' asked Don Camillo between clenched teeth.

'Babila,' the mother answered defiantly.

'That won't do,' said Don Camillo.

'And why not?' said the mother with a sarcastic laugh. 'Just because our Party fished the saint out of the river?'

'No,' said Don Camillo glumly. 'Because Babila is a man's name.'

The woman shook her head and turned to look at the saint. On the base was printed: 'Saint Babila, B –'

'Saint Babila, Blessed, I suppose,' she said, laughing again.

'No,' said Don Camillo, 'that *B* is for "Bishop".'

The mother, the godparents, and their friends looked at one another disappointedly.

'A bishop!' the mother muttered ill-humouredly. 'We might as well have left him at the bottom of the river!'

'Very well, then,' said Don Camillo, grinding his teeth; 'what's to be the name?'

The little group wore a puzzled air.

'Palmira, like our leader, Palmiro Togliatti,' one suggested.

'Marilyn,' said the godmother, who was a passionate reader of film magazines.

And Marilyn it was.

Peppone's Pilgrimage

SELDOM had there been such a miserable autumn; when it didn't rain cats and dogs, it drizzled. If, by virtue of some miracle, the sun peeped out in the morning, by afternoon there was a fog thick enough to be cut with a knife and even wetter than water. The ground was damp and rotted, and the peasants were at their wit's end because they saw no prospect of sowing the wheat. Mules and oxen sank up to their bellies in the lush grass, and tractor wheels could only spin idly, becoming more and more heavily weighed down with mud. No one but a madman would have ventured out if he didn't have to, that is, no one but a madman or a hunter, because a hunter is only a madman who hasn't been shut up in an institution.

On this mid-November afternoon a hunter was walking, or rather ploughing his way, along the Canal. He wore high rubber boots, and every now and then he had to stop and wipe them, because the mud stuck to them and pulled him down. He hadn't yet fired a single shot and it seemed unlikely that he would fire one, but he continued to trudge along, accompanied by a totally unenthusiastic dog. At a certain point the dog was so disgusted that he turned round and started for home.

'Thunder!'

The dog stopped, looked round at his master, and trotted farther away.

'Thunder! Come here!'

The hunter's voice was charged with anger, and the dog finally went to him, growling.

'As long as I'm here, you've got to stick by me,' he said, as the dog came near.

And if the dog could have spoken he would doubtless have said:

'Just because you're a jackass, Reverend, doesn't mean that I have to be one too!'

Don Camillo continued to mutter under his breath for a while, and then, when the fog began to close in around him, he decided that Thunder's idea wasn't such a bad one, after all. After a decent silence, he said:

'If you want to go home, run along. I'm tired of having you underfoot.'

He shot the last round from his shotgun and hung it, with the barrel pointing down, under his heavy coat, from the right shoulder. Just then Thunder pricked up his ears, moved a few feet forward, and stiffened all over.

'Why did it have to be just now?' grumbled Don Camillo, reaching under his coat for the gun.

But hardly had he extricated it than he realized that Thunder was pointing to no ordinary game, for he was barking, in deep, gloomy tones, in the direction of a clump of acacias. Don Camillo attempted to quiet him and then took up his stand behind a mulberry tree. He saw the acacia branches move, and a moment later there appeared a shadowy, tall human figure, without a head, advancing slowly upon him. All of a sudden Thunder leaped forward, barking joyfully now, as if in recognition. Don Camillo saw that this was no headless ghost, but a big man, holding a coat over his head. Actually, the coat was over the head of the child he was carrying on his shoulders.

'For a minute I thought you were a man without a head,' said Don Camillo, when the giant stopped in front of him. 'And considering the little use that head of yours is to you, I wasn't so very far wrong.'

The man stuck his head out from the folds of the coat.

'Father,' he said, 'if it weren't for the respect I bear your dog, I'd give you the answer you deserve.'

'Take it easy, Peppone,' Don Camillo said with a laugh. 'I didn't mean to insult you.'

'I shall insult you, though, Father, if you don't remove yourself and let an honest man go his way.'

'Strictly speaking, you're not going your way; you're poaching on someone else's property. But, be that as it may, no one is stopping you.'

'Then, Father, don't block the whole path; I don't want to wet my feet in the grass. Instead of wasting your dog's time, you'd do better to go and pray to your Boss to send us a bit of sun!'

'My Boss needs no advice from me,' said Don Camillo, stepping aside. 'He knows when to make the sun shine or the rain fall.'

'It doesn't seem that way to me,' said Peppone, starting to walk along. 'Your Boss goes in for politics instead of attending to business.'

Don Camillo did not bother to reply, but slung his gun over his shoulder and walked along, behind Peppone. Once they had left the Canal, Peppone said, without turning round:

'How much longer are you going to trail me?'

'I'm going my own way,' Don Camillo replied. 'A hunter's way is through the open fields. But, if I may ask, where are *you* going?'

'Where I please,' shouted back Peppone. 'Hasn't anyone a right to find the fields open but you?'

'Yes,' said Don Camillo. 'But I have a right to find it

very odd indeed that a man should go walking in the mud with a five-year-old child on his shoulders who would be much better off at home.'

'My son is my own concern,' roared Peppone. 'Kindly keep your mind on your own affairs!'

'That's just the point. I baptized him and entered him in my books. That's why I have a right to say that your head must be full of cotton-wool if you carry him around on a day like this.'

Peppone did not answer, because just then he slipped in the mud and would have fallen to the ground had not Don Camillo bolstered him up from behind.

'Do you see what I mean?' the priest asked him. 'You might have knocked his brains out.'

'It's all your fault!' shouted Peppone, stamping his feet in order to shake off some of the mud that had stuck to them. 'You needle me until I can't see where I'm going.'

Don Camillo opened his coat, took off his shotgun, and set it up against another mulberry tree.

'Give the child to me, while you wipe your big horse-shoes,' he said, lifting the burden from Peppone's shoulders.

Peppone cursed to himself as he plucked a branch and angrily scraped the mud off his boots. It was a tedious job, and the little boy whispered restlessly into Don Camillo's ear:

'Piggy-back, please!'

'Be quiet!' said Don Camillo gruffly.

The little boy pouted and made as if to cry. In order to avoid a scene, Don Camillo lifted him up to his shoulders. As he raised his arms his coat started to slip off, and he stopped it only by leaning against a tree.

'Catch it, will you?' he shouted to Peppone.

'Catch what?' asked Peppone aggressively.

'My coat. It's about to fall into the mud.'

Peppone stopped scraping and went to pick up the

coat. From the priest's shoulders the little boy signalled to his father, pointing repeatedly at his own head.

'No,' said Peppone. 'Wait till I take you back. He wouldn't like it.'

'What wouldn't I like?' roared Don Camillo.

'For him to put your coat over his head.'

'Go on, throw it over his head, and hurry up with what you're doing,' said Don Camillo, holding fast to the little legs that swung down over his chest.

Peppone threw the coat over the child's head, and for a minute the priest's eyes were covered. When he had parted the folds and looked out he saw Peppone balancing unsteadily on one foot and then falling backwards into a puddle.

'Neat work!' the priest exclaimed. 'If the cells of your Party are as solid as the cornerstone, then the revolution will be here soon!'

'If your hind quarters were as wet as mine,' Peppone grumbled, 'you'd display a little more Christian charity!'

He struggled to his feet and came over to take back his son, but Don Camillo stepped away.

'Leave him with me,' he said; 'with my rubber boots I'm not so likely to stumble. Take my gun, and when we reach the road I'll turn over this little monkey to you.'

'I'm not going to the road,' said Peppone glumly.

'Then where are you going?'

'I'm going where I see fit. Give me back my boy and let me alone.'

Don Camillo peered out from among the folds of his coat at Peppone.

'Look here, wild man, this child has a raging fever. If you don't take him straight home . . .'

'Taking him home wouldn't help,' muttered Peppone. 'For two months now it's come on him every evening, and the doctor can't find a cure. Give him back and stop bothering me!'

'*Quo vadis*, Peppone?' asked Don Camillo, shaking his head.

'*Quo vadis* wherever I please, and *quo venisti*, too, in spite of all the cursed clergy in the world put together! I'm going where I have to go.'

'Can't you go by the road?'

'No, I tell you! I have to cross the fields. I don't mind humbling myself before Almighty God, but I won't be a laughing-stock of priests and priest's pets.'

Don Camillo looked hard at Peppone's agonized face.

'Very well, I won't say another word. Let's get going.'

'I'll carry the child.'

'No; he's safer on my shoulders. And no use carrying the shotgun. We may as well leave it here and Thunder will keep watch over it.'

The fog had closed in on them and it was wetter and wetter underfoot, but they kept on walking. For part of the way they moved in a direction parallel to that of the road, but neither of them mentioned it. The distance of seven miles seemed interminable. Finally, just before the fog made everything invisible they arrived at their destination. It was a big brick building, darkened by age, which rose at one side of a little-travelled road, with barren fields, where once upon a time rice had grown, all round it. Three hundred years earlier it had been a mere chapel, but later it had become the sanctuary of the Madonna of the Fields. Peppone, with a rough gesture, took his son into his arms.

'You stay outside,' he said brusquely to Don Camillo. 'I don't want you spying on me.'

Don Camillo waited at the door, while Peppone hoisted the little boy on to his shoulders and went in. The church was cold and half-dark, and not a soul was there. The Madonna of the Fields was the only living thing, with her eyes gleaming from above the altar. Don Camillo kept watch at the door. For several minutes he knelt down on a stone and told the Madonna all the things that Peppone probably didn't know how to tell her. When he heard the door creak he got up.

'If you have anything to say, you can go in now,' said Peppone.

'I've had my say already,' said Don Camillo.

And they started back across the fields, with the child under the coat, on Don Camillo's shoulders. The fog was so thick that towards the end they nearly lost their way. Don Camillo whistled, and Thunder came to guide them. It was dark when they reached the rectory, and Peppone said:

'I'll take back my load.'

He slipped off Don Camillo's coat, and saw that the child's head was reclining on his.

'The little fellow's asleep,' he murmured.

'Not as fast asleep as you might think,' said Don Camillo.

'What do you mean?'

'If your neck were as wet as mine, you wouldn't have to ask,' said Don Camillo, handing the child over.

Peppone stood for a moment as if he had something important to say, but could not find the words.

'I hope you won't go around telling how we tough Reds go back in an emergency to ... our childhood,' said Peppone hopefully.

'I'm no tell-tale,' said Don Camillo. 'But if only you weren't such a silly fellow ...'

'Don't ask the impossible,' said Peppone firmly.

Don Camillo ran to kneel down in front of the main altar.

'Forgive me, Lord,' he said, 'if I wasn't here for vespers.'

'Absence excused!' Christ said with a smile.

The New Look

WHEN the official news came through, along with the first directives, Peppone was staggered. In the good old days he had fought like a lion to have one of the village streets called after Joseph Stalin and had even given his name to the Consumer's Co-operative. As if this were not enough, the great hall of his emporium and meeting-place was decorated with a bigger-than-life-size portrait of the great man.

Such was Peppone's discomfiture that when he had called his henchmen together he found himself for the first time with nothing to say. All he did was toss the sheet of paper containing the directives on to the table and throw out his arms in a helpless and disconsolate manner. The others read the paper through and looked at one another. Then Smilzo summed up the situation.

'What fault have we, Chief, if we believed what the higher-ups told us? Anyhow, it's all perfectly simple. We take down the street sign, change the Co-operative's name, and splash a bucket of whitewash over that wall. Stalinism has gone down the drain.'

They had met in the Co-operative, and on the wall in front of them was the gigantic portrait of the moustachioed, posthumously purged Leader. Peppone looked at it very sadly. He suffered not only from the blow to his faith, but from a vivid memory of the amount of money the portrait had cost. He himself had insisted that it be a fresco, because, as he had declared at the unveiling, 'it must endure as long as the glory of the father of all peoples, that is, forever and ever'.

In the great hall were gathered only Peppone and his general staff; the hoi polloi were playing cards and listening to the radio in two other rooms. Thus they were spared the sight of the discredited leader, while Peppone and his intimates could discuss the situation more freely. Naturally enough, when Don Camillo's voice suddenly boomed forth in their midst they started as if a cannon had sounded.

'Good evening,' he said heartily, and went to sit down at a small table.

'This hall is reserved for private deliberations,' Smilzo told him.

Don Camillo settled back in his chair, stuck a cigar butt between his lips, and calmly lit it.

'Is there some celebration?' he asked, after he had blown a smoke-ring up at the ceiling.

'When a visitor sees that he's not wanted,' put in Peppone, 'the least he can do is go away without stopping to argue.'

'Certainly,' said Don Camillo. 'But when a visitor is taking advantage of his last chance to admire a masterpiece of art which is about to be destroyed, then, wanted or not wanted, it's his duty to remain.'

He scrutinized the painting on the wall with a connoisseur's eye and then ended:

'Because it's a fresco, you'll have to scrape and replaster the wall. Twelve square yards of plastering are no joke.'

There was no reply. Peppone clenched his fists but held his tongue.

'Oh well, politics is politics. I don't run the same risk, thank heaven. My Leader's held his own for nearly two thousand years.'

Peppone jumped to his feet.

'Father,' he said, 'if you want to pick a fight, you've come to the right place.'

Don Camillo shook his head.

'Never again, Mr Mayor, never again! We've fought quite often enough over that fellow with the bushy moustache. I came simply to indulge in the legitimate satisfaction of seeing you destroy the image of your former god.'

Peppone brought his fist down on the table and shouted:

'You shan't have that satisfaction!'

Again Don Camillo shook his head.

'Mr Mayor, you've misunderstood me. I don't say that you must take a hammer and start to knock off the plaster in my sight. I just want to know that you've given orders for the demolition. Farewell, Face! . . .'

Peppone brought down his other fist on the table.

'I'm giving no such orders. As long as I live, that face won't be touched.'

'Then you're disobeying the higher-ups. You're running foul of Party discipline.'

'No, I'm not,' shouted Peppone. 'The Party doesn't order me to give satisfaction to a rascally priest or other such garbage.'

When Don Camillo had left home it wasn't with the intention of getting Peppone into so much trouble, but now that things had taken this turn he let him stew in his own juice.

'Well, do as you see fit,' he retorted blandly. 'But at least I'll have the satisfaction of seeing Stalin's name obliterated from the façade of the Co-operative and the street sign.'

'You shan't see anything at all!' shouted Peppone.

Peppone got into really hot water because the reactionary papers took up the story and carried pieces about 'deviations', 'Stalinist factions', and 'possible splits'. Very soon a bright young man was sent from national headquarters. He called a meeting of Peppone's chief henchmen and addressed them as follows:

'The reactionary papers are printing the usual absurd stories, but there's no use contradicting them. The only answer is to go ahead and get rid of the painting and the street sign and the name on the façade of the building, as originally intended.'

The man from headquarters was a stickler for discipline, the sort of young Party worker that wears spectacles and a double-breasted suit. But he made no impression on Peppone.

'My personal prestige is at stake,' Peppone told him. 'We're not getting rid of anything. I won't hear of giving that miserable priest such satisfaction.'

The man from headquarters tried to explain that where the dignity of the Party is involved, that of the individual must take second place. He brought in the dangers of the 'personality cult' and its terrible consequences. Then, when he saw that Peppone was still looking askance at him, he thought up a compromise solution.

'Comrade, I know how to reconcile our points of view. We'll send you off on a mission, and while you're away, your men will obey our orders to wipe everything out.'

Bigio was a man of few words, and those he did speak tumbled out of his mouth like bricks falling from the top of a scaffolding.

'It will have to be *your* men that carry out *your* orders. We're not wiping out a thing. You got us into all this trouble. Why couldn't you tell us before he died just how things stood?'

The man from headquarters looked round and then

25

explained that he was only a link in the chain of command.

'Very well, then,' he concluded. 'I'll make a report on your objections.'

He did exactly this, and as a result Peppone received an ultimatum; either to knuckle under or else to be expelled from the Party for indiscipline and other damaging reasons.

It was a peremptory letter, and having read it several times Peppone went to the rectory and threw it down in front of Don Camillo. Don Camillo read it over and over in his turn and then came out with the single word:

'Garibaldi.'

'Garibaldi?' muttered Peppone suspiciously. 'Where does he come in?'

'Because he has the same first name as Stalin, and you can leave the first half of the inscription on the façade of the Co-operative the way it is. As for the painting, you don't need to deface it. You can just pierce a hole and put in a glass door connecting the great hall with the pergola and the bowling-alley. As for the street sign, never mind about that. One day it will fall, all by itself.'

Peppone pounded his fists on the table and thrust his chin out in the direction of Don Camillo.

'I said I wasn't going to give you any satisfaction!'

'I don't want any. You've won, and this is my surrender. You're the stronger of the two.'

'Father, I can't trust you. There's something here that doesn't meet the eye.'

'Only a little common sense,' said Don Camillo, shaking his head. 'I'd rather have a live Peppone than a dead Stalin. It's better to thumb a nose at Stalin than at you. Just think it over and see if you don't agree.'

Peppone thought for a moment, and then said:

'From my point of view, you're quite right.'

'From mine too. . . . Lambrusco wine or Fontanella?'

'Lambrusco,' said Peppone without hesitation.

It was an usually fine bottle and so were the two that followed. At a certain point Peppone raised his glass and shouted:

'Hurrah for Garibaldi!'

'Hurrah!' said Don Camillo, clinking his glass against the other.

Then they had to drink a toast to the conscripts born in 1899, iron men, one and all.

'We ninety-niners!...' exclaimed Peppone.

And he said these three words in such a way that they were as meaningful as a long oration.

The Case of the Disappearing Dog

DON CAMILLO's dog, Thunder, had fallen from grace, and was punished by being tied up, for several weeks, on a chain. Just when it seemed as if he had mended his ways he made for the garden gate, returned to the gay life, and for several days on end failed to put in an appearance.

'The fact that the hunting season is over doesn't dispense you from the everyday duties of a well-bred dog,' said Don Camillo. 'You're not a mutt or a stray, you have a pedigree. *Noblesse oblige*, and although you're quite free to go out by yourself, you must come home at night.'

Thunder cocked his head and listened with a penitent air, but these high-sounding words went in one ear and out the other. Don Camillo was genuinely fearful of losing his beloved pet. Even the loss of his indispensable motorcycle would have been less difficult to bear. But fate willed, perversely, that Don Camillo should lose his dog. Thunder disappeared on Saturday morning while Don Camillo was saying his first mass. For a couple of days the priest hoped for his return, then he betrayed his worry by making inquiries of his neighbours. No one in the village had seen him, and gradually Don Camillo extended his search to the outlying farms.

Actually, his first thought had been to question Peppone, for Peppone was the only other person for whom Thunder felt affection. One day Peppone had even gone so far as to say: 'Politics may divide us, but Thunder makes us one. Nevertheless, come the revolution, Thunder won't save you from the fate you so richly deserve!' Now Peppone was just the man to whom Don Camillo wanted to turn, but the political situation was unusually tense, and if he had made any contact with the Red leader, an earthquake might have ensued. In the long run, however, after he had exhausted all other possibilities, Don Camillo did have to knock at Peppone's door, that is he wrote him a letter.

Dear Mr Giuseppe Bottazzi:

My dog, Thunder, has been missing for two weeks past. If you can give me any news of him, I shall be most grateful. Yours very truly . . .

The answer came by return of post:

Dear Mr Priest:

If your dog has run away, it means that he, too, has got wise to you. Very truly yours . . .

Don Camillo did not abandon his quest, and after a month had gone by he asked Barchini to print fifty notices, which he proceeded to post in the surrounding district:

Lost: Hunting dog. Reward to anyone bringing information which leads to his return.

After three days Don Camillo received a missive with crudely printed letters and no signature at the bottom:

Reverend: If you want to find your dog, without having to give any reward, go to the acacia grove at Pragrande and look in the vicinity of the sewer.

Without losing a single minute, Don Camillo set out across the fields in the direction of Pragrande. He didn't have to look far, because near the sewer entrance there was a pole sticking out of the ground, with a dog-collar wired to it, and a crudely printed sign saying:

Here lies one of the two dogs of the rectory. He was run over by a truck: too bad, because the other one is more of a dog than he.

With his stick Don Camillo dug up the loose earth round the pole. After he had gone down a couple of feet he replaced the dirt and went away. Back in the rectory he shut himself up in his bedroom in order to quiet the sorrow and indignation that welled up in his breast. Turning the collar over and over in his hands he repeated to himself: 'They killed him . . . they killed him. . . .' There was no doubt in his mind: out of sheer spite, someone had murdered the dog. But who could it be? In spite of his resentment, Don Camillo could not bear to think that the murderer was someone he knew. No one in the village could have been so vile. There were people who might have killed a man, but never a dog, just in order to hurt the master. All day long he was in the dumps, and when evening came he was as exhausted as if he had unloaded a transatlantic steamer. He had no wish to talk, and when he went to close the church and found the old Desolina Fiorini waiting to see him he started to dismiss her roughly.

'Father,' she said mysteriously, 'I have a secret to tell you.'

'What is it?' asked Don Camillo curtly.

'I read the notice about the dog. . . .'

'Well . . .' said Don Camillo, taken by surprise.

'It's no use your offering a reward. Someone knows where the dog is, but he's not talking.'

'Well, you can talk, can't you?' panted Don Camillo. 'Don't you trust me?'

'I trust you, Father, but I don't want to get in trouble with those people. . . .'

'What people?'

'The usual people, Father. Didn't the dog disappear on the twenty-fourth of last month?'

'Yes.'

'Well, I saw him with one of them on that day.'

Don Camillo could contain himself no longer. The old woman's caution was driving him crazy. Still, it would have been unwise to put too much pressure upon her.

'Speak up, Desolina,' he said. 'After all, you know me.'

'I know them, too. . . . This wasn't the first time your dog had gone out with them, either. First he took up with the ringleader; he was always underfoot in the workshop. After that he shifted his attentions to the ringleader's right-hand man. I must admit I was shocked to see the company your dog was keeping.'

'They made the overtures,' protested Don Camillo. 'And what does he know of politics?'

'Nothing, of course, Father. But I know that it could only come to a bad end. Anyone that takes up with the Reds . . .'

'Desolina,' said Don Camillo prudently, 'when you speak of "the ringleader's right-hand man", do you mean Smilzo?'

'Yes,' she said unwillingly, after a fearful look around her. 'That was his special friend. I saw them go off more than once together, on Peppone's truck. . . . On the twenty-fourth of last month, which was a Saturday, that's exactly what happened. Only that time Smilzo came back alone.'

Don Camillo had heard all too much. After reassuring the old woman, he went back to the rectory and brooded over his wrong in bed. He slept very little, rose at dawn, and as soon as he had said mass made straight for the workshop of Peppone. It looked suspiciously like a co-incidence that Smilzo should be on the scene as well. But Peppone was obviously unprepared to see Don Camillo turn up at this early hour and with such an angry look on his face.

'Did you have a bad night, Father?' he asked.

'I did. But I slept better than someone with a dung-heap where a conscience should be.'

'For instance? . . .' asked Peppone threateningly.

'For instance the fellow who murdered my dog simply in order to spite me.'

Peppone shook his head.

'The loss of the dog has affected his mind,' he muttered. 'There's nothing to do but let him have his say. He's dreamed that somebody killed the dog and come to tell us about it instead of going to a soothsayer who might have interpreted the dream in terms of a winning lottery number.'

'I didn't dream it at all,' said Don Camillo, pulling Thunder's collar out of his pocket, along with the letter and sign. 'I found him dead over at Pragrande, with this sign for a tombstone.'

Peppone read both documents.

'Too bad,' he said. 'But you're barking up the wrong tree. Here there are people that would have been glad to kill you in order to please the dog, but none that would have killed the dog just to spite you.'

'This isn't the wrong tree at all,' Don Camillo insisted. 'I'm looking for a fellow who on the twenty-fourth of last month rode off on the truck belonging to a certain Giuseppe Bottazzi, who rode off with my dog and rode back without him.'

Peppone took a step forward.

'You're barking up the wrong tree, Father, I tell you!'

'The police sergeant won't bark up the wrong tree, though, after I've told him my story and given him the names of witnesses.'

'I'm not afraid of you or the police, either. If somebody killed your dog, we can't do anything about it. The sins of priests who have sold their souls to America are visited upon innocent dogs!'

'We'll see who has the last laugh!' shouted Don Camillo, moving towards the door. 'Ten minutes from now there's going to be an H-bomb explosion, and then the fun will begin.'

Smilzo had turned as pale as the lady of the camelias. He grasped Peppone's arm and pleaded.

'Chief, don't let him go!'

But Peppone stared at him in amazement and shook him off.

'What's the matter, you fool?' he asked.

Don Camillo had stopped to look round.

'I'll expose you and your whole miserable gang,' he shouted towards Smilzo. 'No use your putting on an act like that with me.'

'Father, I didn't kill your dog, I swear it!' Smilzo exclaimed.

'Good for you! Then swear that you didn't write this sign and this letter. And while you're at it, swear that you didn't take Thunder away with you on Peppone's truck on the twenty-fourth of last month?'

'I'm not swearing indiscriminately,' Smilzo objected. 'I simply swore that I didn't kill your dog.'

'And what dog is buried at Pragrande, then?'

'I can't tell you,' said Smilzo. 'I found him dead on the road a week ago and buried him there. He looked a lot like Thunder, that's all. Afterwards I wrote you an anonymous letter in order to make you stop whining about your lost dog.'

Peppone took Smilzo by the lapels of his jacket and shook him as if he meant to make a single hash out of brains and belly.

'Come out with the whole story,' he shouted, 'or I'll kill you like a dog.'

After Smilzo had caught his breath, he told everything he knew.

'Thunder and I were great friends. He's a good dog; you'd never suspect he belonged to a priest.'

Don Camillo picked up a hammer.

'Be calm, Father,' said Peppone. 'There's no use scaring an innocent witness like me. ... Go ahead, Smilzo.'

'We were friends, as I say. Every Saturday, when I went round to the markets with Peppone's truck, he came along. Once we stopped in a tavern at Peschetto and a fellow asked me if I'd sell the dog. I said that he wasn't mine, that I'd found him on the road. He said he had to have the dog to go hunting and put a thousand-lira note into my hand. I had had a good bit to drink, so I took it and went away. A mile farther on, I realized what a fool I'd been and started to go back for Thunder. While I was turning round Thunder himself ran up and made a flying leap on to the truck. We stopped at the next tavern along the way and drank up the thousand liras.'

'You lout!' said Don Camillo disgustedly. 'Did you teach him to drink, as well?'

'That was just a manner of speaking. I drank red wine and he ate a dish of red meat, such as I wager he never enjoyed when he was with the clergy.'

'Never mind about the clergy,' said Peppone. 'Tell what you have to tell.'

'There isn't much more,' said Smilzo. 'The following Saturday I thought over what had happened. Before stopping to eat lunch in Fornella I took off the dog's collar, smeared him with mud, and took him in with me on the end of a piece of rope. Of course, the rope was tied around his neck in clerical style, so that it could be slipped off, and I had showed him how to get free. I went to a tavern frequented by hunters and there I found a man who wanted to buy him for two thousand liras. And so on, and so on.'

34

'What do you mean, "and so on"?'

'I mean that I drove a mile or so down the road, stopped, and waited for Thunder to catch up with me. When he came we had another bout of eating and drinking, just as before. In short, I'd found a first-class racket. I sold him, he ran away, and then we split the profits.'

'And did he enjoy this game?'

'Of course he enjoyed it. He hasn't sold his soul to America, like you. He understands the economic situation and the necessity of sharing the wealth.'

Once more Don Camillo picked up the hammer.

'And where is Thunder now?' he demanded.

'Last time I saw him was at Castelmonti, where I sold him for three thousand liras, but he never came back. I suppose he never managed to get away. That's the whole story. I didn't kill him; I only pretended he was dead in order to stop your whining about him.'

'Good enough,' said Don Camillo, waving the card in the air. 'Theft, embezzlement, libel . . .'

Peppone felt he had to step in.

'To say that you're more of a dog than Thunder isn't libel; it's no more than the simple truth.'

'We'll see what the court has to say,' said Don Camillo. 'I for one shan't let you off so easily.'

'For once it's not a matter of politics,' said Peppone. 'Smilzo may have done wrong, but he did it entirely on his own, and with the complicity of your dog, who didn't hesitate to second him. Your legal action is directed at a private individual. If you want to send him to jail, go right ahead.'

Don Camillo brought the hammer down on the anvil.

'I don't want to send anyone to jail. I want my dog! Between a thief who sells another man's dog for three thousand liras and a brute who cheats him by paying only a twentieth of the real value, there's not much to choose. But the dog is mine, and I want him back.'

Peppone took his jacket off the hook and slipped it on.

'Shut your holy mouth,' he said. 'You shall have your dog.' And followed by Smilzo he went out and climbed into his truck.

'I'm coming along,' said Don Camillo.

'To Castelmonti,' said Peppone, as Smilzo took the wheel. 'We'll inquire in the tavern who bought the dog and then ransom him, by fair means or foul.'

The truck speeded over the dusty roads of the lower Po valley in the direction of the distant hills. But after seven or eight miles Smilzo abruptly threw on the brakes.

'What's the matter?' Peppone asked impatiently.

Smilzo opened the door and a dog leaped into the cab. The dog was Thunder. Nobody said a word, and Smilzo turned round and made for home. After a mile the silence was broken by an angry growl and again Smilzo came to a sudden stop.

'What's the matter now?' asked Don Camillo.

'Our understanding is that at the first tavern we stop and divide the spoils,' Smilzo explained. 'I still owe him his share from the last time.'

With Thunder at his heels he got out and went into the tavern in front of which he had stopped the truck. Peppone followed suit, leaving Don Camillo alone. It was as hot as summer, and under the metal top of the cab Don Camillo soon began to perspire. Finally he got out, went into the tavern, and asked for a glass of water.

'Come in, Father,' said the host, going by with a huge bowl of spaghetti in his arms. 'Your friends are waiting for you in the next room.'

The room was shady and quiet, and the spaghetti emanated an ambrosial odour. Don Camillo sat in front of a heaping plateful, and only then did Thunder abandon his reserved air and show his adoration. But Don Camillo was not to be corrupted.

'I'm paying for what I eat,' he said stoutly. 'No dishonestly gained bread for me!'

'Nor for me,' said Peppone. 'Every man must pay for himself, and the devil take the hindmost. But Smilzo's paying for both himself and Thunder.'

'Then I'll pay for you, Peppone,' said Don Camillo. 'That way Smilzo and I shall both have dog guests!'

And he proceeded to enjoy his meal, because having the last word made it worthwhile to pay for an entire regiment.

Victims of War

MILCO didn't know how to begin, but finally he managed to say:

'It's about that German woman. Today is the twenty-sixth, and she'll be here the day after tomorrow.'

He seemed to be intensely worried, and Don Camillo couldn't see why.

'Every twenty-eighth of March since 1946 she's descended upon you. She may just as well come this year, too.'

Milco shook his head.

'You don't know the whole story, Father,' muttered Milco; 'that's why you can't understand.'

True enough, Don Camillo knew no more than did the rest of the village. The story went back to the end of September 1943, when a small detachment of Germans had occupied the village. Among them was Sergeant Fritz, who functioned as quartermaster. He himself was lodged in Milco's house at La Torretta, not very far from the village, between the highway and the Stivone River.

At this time Milco was thirty years old, but he had

stayed at home because of a lame leg and also because, in spite of this disability, he was the only man able to run the farm. Milco's wife was not strong, and his extremely healthy son was only eleven years old. There were no other members of the family, and in time of war, when agriculture is just as important as heavy industry, there can be no question of leaving the land deserted and unproductive.

Sergeant Fritz was a good-natured fellow, the same age as Milco, who went about making war as another man might have gone about store-keeping or accounting. Good German that he was, he had a weakness for Italian wine, and when he had drunk a bit more than necessary he would pull out of his wallet the photograph of a handsome, blonde young woman and a ten-month-old blond baby boy, which invariably moved him to tears.

Sergeant Fritz was happy in Milco's house, and both Milco and his wife treated him like one of the family. He had a happy-go-lucky temperament, and since he was in charge of the commissary department he never came back to the farm empty-handed. The sergeant stayed in Milco's house until 28 March 1945. On the evening of that day he did not come back, and the next day he was fished out of the Stivone River, near Brugello. But it was plain that he had not drowned, for three bullets from a P-38 had gone clean through his head. In those days the Partisans were very active, and Sergeant Fritz had run into one of their bands.

The twenty-eighth of March after the war was over, a blonde young German woman and her blond baby came to La Torretta. The woman knew about four words of Italian and Milco knew about four words of German, so that they were able to understand one another.

'I am the widow of Sergeant Fritz,' she told him, 'and I have come to lay flowers on his tomb.'

Milco took her to the cemetery, and she laid her flowers at the foot of the crude wooden cross on which was written the Sergeant's life story:

Fritz Hauser
2 March 1925–8 March 1945

Milco and his wife asked the woman and her child to stay with them for a whole week. The woman talked about the dreadful conditions in Germany and the difficulties she had encountered on her trip. But above all she talked about Fritz. She said that Fritz had written her a very moving account of Milco and his family, and that she had come not only to visit his tomb but also to pay a tribute of gratitude to them, in short, to thank them for all they had done for her husband.

'I had to sell every last bit of gold I possessed in order to make the journey,' she told them. 'Now I have nothing. But I hope to find a job, so that next year I shall have another money to come see you again.'

She kept her word, and turned up promptly the next year and the one that followed. Punctually, on every twenty-eighth of March, she came with her child to stay for a week at La Torretta. By now everyone in the village knew her and her story. Whenever they met her in the street, they greeted her profusely because, among other things, she was 'a fine figure of a girl'. She had the generously proportioned sort of beauty which is especially appreciated in the fertile Po valley.

Don Camillo was still perplexed.

'I don't see what it is that requires such special understanding,' he muttered. 'No one can criticize you for letting her stay in your house, even if you're a widower. After all, you don't live there alone; you have your son and his policewoman of a wife with you. And your wife – God rest her soul! – was already dead when this German woman came last year. What has happened since then to change the situation?'

Milco hesitated for a moment and then said abruptly:
'I simply don't want to see her again!'

Don Camillo shrugged his shoulders.

'Well, then, why have you come to me? That's none
of my business. If you don't like her face, just write her a
letter and tell her to stay away.'

But Milco had something more on his mind, as was
plain to see from the way he twisted his hat in his hands.

'As long as my wife was alive, I could talk things out
with her. But now, who is there for me to talk to?'

By now the channel of communication was opened,
and Don Camillo had only to let Milco have his say.

'Father, you remember how it was. I was tied up with
the Resistance movement, and they had put me in charge
of transmitting their radio messages. I had the radio
hidden under a barrel in my barn. On that evening of
28 March 1945 Fritz caught me red-handed. . . .'

'Fritz caught you?' stammered Don Camillo.

'Yes. As usual, after we'd finished supper, I said:
"I'm going to have a game of cards with Ronchini."
And as usual, he said: "Good luck to you!" I went out
and started to walk across the fields, but when I reached
the beech-tree I stayed there for a quarter of an hour and
then retraced my steps. There was a little door at the
rear of the barn which I was the only one ever to use. I
slipped through it and took out the transmitting appara-
tus, just as I had done a hundred times before. But this
time the worst possible thing happened: Fritz burst in
and caught me at it. . . .'

He paused and wiped the perspiration off his forehead.

'A light went on, and there was Fritz standing before
me, quite beside himself with rage. "Traitor!" he
shouted, with his hand on the butt of his pistol. I had my
own finger on the trigger of a loaded P-38, which was
always in my pocket, and I beat him to the draw. . . .
Cursed war! . . .'

And he stopped again to wipe his forehead.

'If he hadn't called me "Traitor", perhaps I wouldn't have shot him, but the word sounded like a death sentence. . . . It was dark and rainy outside. I loaded his body on to my shoulders, carried it down to the river, and threw it in. The Stivone was running high and the body was swept a couple of miles downstream, to the place where it was later found. No one had the slightest suspicion. My wife was the only one ever to know, and now she's dead.'

Don Camillo pondered for several minutes over this story. Finally he muttered:

'What can I say? Am I to call you a patriot or an assassin? Your own conscience must be your guide.'

'That's why I'm here,' Milco exclaimed. 'I can't look at it from the patriotic angle. Even if I were to get a medal, I'd still consider myself guilty of murdering Fritz. I can't sleep at night. . . . The first time that German woman came and started to thank me for all I'd done for her dead husband, I thought I'd go through the floor with shame. . . . I killed him and she thanks me! And the fatherless child calls me uncle! No, I can't stand it any longer. I can't live through fifty-one weeks of the year dreading the fifty-second. I don't want ever to see her again; I don't want my stomach to turn over. Father, you can't imagine what I've gone through in the last ten years.'

'Yes, I can imagine,' said Don Camillo. 'And I'm glad that you suffered. It shows that your conscience is working.'

'Yes, it is,' said Milco excitedly. 'That's why I came here. I'm not looking for comfort. You can say what you please, but the fact remains that I murdered Fritz. You'll have to help me shake off that woman. I haven't the heart to do it, but surely you can tell her the whole story.'

'I?' exclaimed Don Camillo, with wide-open eyes.

'Yes. She's arriving the day after tomorrow. You must

talk to her. . . . It isn't right that she should thank me for my kindness and treat me like a friend. I'm taking something that isn't due. She must be told that I killed her husband, and then she must tell her son. That way she'll never come back, and my sufferings will be at an end.'

Don Camillo shook his head.

'No, Milco, if you really have a conscience, then you mustn't seek to evade further suffering. It's not enough to repent; you must make amends as well. If the sight of this woman makes you suffer, then you must thank God for letting you see her. And why should you wish to hurt her still more? Aren't you satisfied with having killed her husband?'

Milco waved his arms wildly.

'Of course I don't want to hurt her!'

'Well, that's just what you're going to do. She trusts you and thinks of you as one of the family, and you'd rob her of this last illusion. If her presence gives you pain, so much the better. I'll say a prayer for you.'

After Milco had gone away, Don Camillo went into the church to pray for him. But it was a very strange prayer.

'Lord,' Don Camillo said to the Christ on the altar, 'in this filthy land, there are tens of thousands of persons who killed tens of thousands of others. And they're not sorry; in fact, they brag about it. They want medals and positions; they want to be deputies to parliament, senators, and publishers; they want their pictures in the school-books of the nation! . . . Now here's a poor devil who has suffered ten years just because he killed a man, and we are powerless to help him. We can't say: "Look here, Milco. . . . When Fritz caught you with the radio, he called you a traitor, didn't he? Well, you could have called him the same thing! While you were in the barn working for the Resistance Movement, your wife, abetted by Sergeant Fritz, was working for Germany . . . without thought of resistance!" ... No, Lord, we can't tell this to Milco, because his wife revealed it on her death-bed, and a priest can't violate the secret of the confessional. Lord, You know best, but is it right, I ask you?'

'Yes, it is, Don Camillo,' Christ answered. 'The sin of the wife doesn't cancel the sin of the husband. Each one has to pay. . . .'

March 28 rolled round, and with it came the Germans. As soon as Don Camillo heard of their arrival he hurried out to La Torretta, where Milco greeted him like a long-lost friend. It was a fine, sunny day and while the little boy played in the yard with the dog, his mother, Milco, and Don Camillo went to look at the fields, which were just stirring from their long hibernation.

'You haven't much colour in your cheeks,' said Don Camillo to the German woman.

'I work at a factory in a big city, where there's lots of smoke,' she explained.

'That's no good,' said Don Camillo gravely. 'And don't you have to pinch and scrape all year in order to make this visit?'

'I don't mind pinching and scraping,' she answered with a smile.

'Why don't you come and live here, near Fritz?' said Don Camillo. 'That would make Fritz happy, I'm sure.'

She stared at him in amazement.

'Don't you like it here?' Don Camillo asked her.

'Oh, very much! Italy is the most wonderful place! But I have a home and a job. . . .'

Don Camillo waved in the direction of Milco's house.

'Why not have a home and a job here?'

Don Camillo had no gift for parlour games, and so he came straight to the point:

'You marry him . . . he marries you . . . I perform the ceremony . . . that way everyone will be happy!'

The woman was thirty-seven years old, but she still

knew how to blush and proceeded to do so. Milco was forty-two and too old for blushing, but he turned pale. Don Camillo was no matchmaker, and now embarrassment overcame him.

'Very well,' he said. 'Think it over. When you're ready you'll find me in my office. *Guten Abend.*'

And with that he went away.

Apparently they did think it over, for three days later Milco came to see him.

'Well, Father, you shall have your way, and we'll get married.'

'Exactly. It's your way, too, I trust.'

Milco heaved a sigh.

'Here's hoping that to have her around all the time won't give me more pain than ever. If my conscience still hurts me . . .'

'Let's get this straight, Milco,' said Don Camillo. 'Where Fritz is concerned, things are just the same. You took away his life, and you can't restore it. That will have to stay on your conscience. But when it comes to the woman and child, it's a different matter. You deprived her of her husband, but you're giving her another . . . and there'll no longer be a fatherless boy. Don't mix your accounts!'

'God help me, that's all I can say!' exclaimed Milco.

'He's helped you already!' retorted Don Camillo.

Stranded in the Stratosphere

When the Carnival came for the mid-May holiday that year, the tents had to be pitched on the grounds that usually served as a livestock market. The whole region was in a political ferment and the Left-wingers planned to hold a series of meetings in the village square.

The carnival's improvised pitch was out of the way, on the outskirts of the village, along the road to Molinetto. But there were two startling new attractions: a big auto-drome and a stratospheric merry-go-round. The strato-spheric merry-go-round was a cornucopia of steel rods resembling the skeleton of an inverted umbrella. At the top end of every rod, there was a miniature aeroplane, and when the merry-go-round revolved, every rider could raise or lower his vehicle by simply pressing a lever.

The rectory was no more than three or four hundred yards away, and every evening, when Don Camillo retired to his room, on the second floor, he looked for half an hour or so out of the window at the revolving merry-go-round before drawing the curtain and going to bed.

There is nothing in the least sinful about riding on a merry-go-round, either on the ground or in the air, but it is an amusement in which a priest cannot indulge. People have eyes to see and not much grey matter for thinking, and the sight of a priest on a merry-go-round would surely rouse them to derision. All this Don Camillo ruefully understood.

The autodrome and the stratospheric merry-go-round were the carnival's two great money-makers, and late in the evening, when the other attractions had closed down, they continued to draw the crowd. And the merry-go-round stayed open longest of all. Don Camillo did not fail to notice this fact, and one fine evening, after the autodrome had stopped running, he went downstairs and out of the house and walked, in a studiedly indifferent manner, across the alfalfa field behind the rectory. When he had reached the hedge bordering the Molinetto road he stood behind it and bided his time. Across the way, the carnival booths lay in darkness, with only the merry-go-round, in the centre of a small island of light, still turning.

Don Camillo's plan was eminently simple. As soon as the last load of riders had dismounted and started home to bed, he would come out from behind the hedge and ask the proprietor to let him enjoy a ride. He did not have long to wait before the merry-go-round came to a halt and a group of young fellows got down, leaped on to their motor-scooters, and rode noisily away into the night. Don Camillo stepped across the ditch and walked straight towards his goal. The proprietor of the merry-go-round, who had stepped into the cabin to count his receipts, jumped when the great dark mass appeared before him.

'First priest you've ever seen?' asked Don Camillo.

'No, Father, but the first one I've ever seen out at this late hour. What can I do for you?'

'I sleep over there,' said Don Camillo, pointing to the

rectory, 'and you've no idea of how your cursed music disturbs me.'

'I'm truly sorry,' said the man, throwing out his arms to signify that there was nothing he could do about it. 'But a merry-go-round without music would be a funereal affair. Late in the evening, I turn the volume very low, but after dark the slightest sound seems to be booming.'

'I quite agree,' said Don Camillo. 'But after you've upset so many of my evenings you ought to be ready to do me a favour.'

'Certainly, Father; anything you say.'

'Then give me a ride on your machine. And I mean right away.'

The proprietor assumed a sincerely regretful air.

'Father, I'll have to ask you to be patient. I'm waiting for a group that arranged to have a couple of rides all together. There they are now.'

Don Camillo wheeled round with the intention of making his escape, but it was too late. The group was directly behind him, and at its head stood Peppone.

'Our beloved parish priest!' he exclaimed. 'Were you expounding the view that it's a mortal sin to ride on the merry-go-round?'

'No, I was simply saying that the music keeps honest folks from sleeping.'

'Oh, is that it? I thought for a minute that *you* were the one that couldn't sleep.'

Smilzo, Bigio, Brusco, Lungo, and Fulmine, in short all the rest of the gang, had paid no attention to the encounter but were gaily clambering into their seats in the planes.

'And what has brought you here, Mr Mayor?' asked Don Camillo in his turn. 'Did you come to give your bad boys some wholesome recreation?'

'Come on, Chief!' called out Smilzo from the merry-go-round.

'Go along, Mr Mayor,' said the smiling Don Camillo. 'The bad boys are calling. What fun to see such a great hulk of a mayor flying a miniature plane!'

'Not half as much fun as to see a great hulk of a priest like yourself at the same occupation!' Peppone retorted.

'The fact is, however, that I shall see a flying mayor, but you're not going to see a flying priest.'

'Well, enjoy the sight while you can,' roared Peppone, striding towards the merry-go-round. 'And don't fail to write a sensational article about it in the scandal sheet with which you plaster the village walls.'

Peppone hoisted himself into a plane while the proprietor prepared to start up the motor, which was inside the cabin.

'Have fun, Father!' repeated Peppone. 'Tell all your good little boys and girls that the Communist administration is spending the taxpayers' money on nocturnal orgies!'

The motor began to run, and out of a loudspeaker came the muted notes of a sprightly march.

'Give her gas, boss!' shouted Peppone, as his plane swung in front of the cabin. 'That way the good Father will have a lullaby to put him to sleep.'

'Shut your big trap!' sounded a voice directly behind him, and when Peppone turned round he saw that Don Camillo was in the plane following his.

By now the merry-go-round was turning at full speed and everyone was having a good time. But soon the damp night air got the better of Don Camillo.

'Tell that fellow down there to go a little more slowly,' he shouted to Peppone.

Peppone pressed the lever and his plane dipped down. As it swung past the cabin he started to call out, but the words stuck in his throat.

'What about it?' shouted Don Camillo.

Peppone muttered something unintelligible and pointed to the cabin. Then Don Camillo went down in his turn and caught sight of what had startled Peppone. What he caught sight of was this: three men with handkerchiefs over their faces, all the way up to the eyes, and revolvers in their hands. The proprietor stood facing the wall and the three men were pushing the barrels of their revolvers into his back, while a fourth one of them dipped into the cash-register drawer and transferred handfuls of paper money to a brief-case. Meanwhile the merry-go-round was whirling at full speed, to the customary musical accompaniment.

The robbers were not satisfied with what they had taken, and two of them went with the proprietor to the trailer where he had his sleeping quarters in order to dig out something more. When they came out they were more dissatisfied than ever and began to manhandle their victim.

'It's no use insisting,' he protested. 'I took the rest of the money to the bank this morning. Look in my wallet and you'll find a receipt for it.'

They found it and tore it angrily into a thousand pieces. And the merry-go-round kept on turning.

'Stop this thing, blast you!' shouted Smilzo as he passed by.

One of the bandits aimed a revolver threateningly in his direction and all the members of Peppone's flying squad pressed their levers simultaneously until the little planes were every one high flying. At this point the merry-go-round really looked like an umbrella turned inside out by the wind. The bandits were furious that their haul was so meagre, but their leader had an abundance of bright ideas.

'We'll separate those fools up there from their money,' he suggested, and raised his face to shout in their direction:

'Empty your pockets, or else we'll shoot the brains out of you.'

'Go to hell!' answered Peppone.

The leader gave an order to his second-in-command, who went into the cabin and turned a handle which caused the planes to whirl faster. Peppone's men cried out, but the bandits' third-in-command turned up the music until it drowned their cries. After half a dozen rounds, the leader jerked his head and the second-in-command brought the velocity to a little less than it had been before.

'Put your money in your handkerchiefs, knot them, and then, when you pass in front of the cabin, throw them in. I'm giving you exactly half a minute to do what I say.'

When the half-minute was up, he went on:

'Beginning with that fellow all in black, start throwing them in!'

Don Camillo, who was obviously the one answering this description, took what little money he had in his pocket and threw his knotted handkerchief into the cabin, and the others followed his example. The bandit leader picked them up and counted the money.

'Too little!' he shouted. 'Throw your wallets with all the rest in them, or else I'll step up the speed. . . . I give you exactly five seconds. Beginning with that fellow all in black, start throwing them in!' Don Camillo, knowing he had practically nothing in his wallet and feeling that this was certainly one time that the poverty of the clergy paid off, threw his wallet. The others followed somewhat more reluctantly but soon seven wallets landed at the leader's feet; they were duly emptied and tossed into a corner. Then the leader turned to the proprietor.

'Don't stop that merry-go-round until a quarter of an hour after we've gone. And you'd better not try to double-cross us, because we'll know how to find you again. We'll set your whole outfit on fire and roast you alive.'

Then the four of them ran for the car they had left on the road and drove away at top speed.

'Stop us, damn you!' shouted the high flyers to the proprietor below. But he was shaking with fear and let the merry-go-round run for the full quarter of an hour which had been enjoined upon him. Then the motor came slowly to a stop and the umbrella gradually closed. The seven took twenty minutes to collect sufficient strength to get out of their planes. Finally they joined the proprietor in the cabin and picked up the empty wallets from the floor. So far, no one had said a word, and now Peppone was the first to speak, grasping the lapels of the proprietor as he did so.

'If you breathe a word of what went on here tonight, I'll not only smash your head, but I'll see to it that you can't hold your carnival in any of the villages in our control.'

'And those in *our* control won't have you either,' added Don Camillo.

Then all seven of them trudged across the field together. Behind the rectory they said good-bye.

'When all is said and done, we had a very pleasant if somewhat expensive evening, did we not, Mr Mayor?' said Don Camillo.

Peppone answered him with a roar which shattered the velvety stillness of the night and roused echoes miles and miles away.

Don Camillo slept well that night, dreaming of a heavenly merry-go-round which transformed even the most black-hearted customers into little children roaring with delight.

The Rains Came

THE weather continued to be wretchedly unseasonable.
After a few sunny days, just enough for the ground to
begin to dry, there came another downpour. It had
started raining early in July of the preceding year, just
when the wheat most needed sun. Then, when the wheat
crop was practically ruined, the implacable rain went on
to kill off the grapes. There was no opportunity to do the
regular autumnal sowing, and immediately after Christ-
mas, when the rain finally stopped, it was followed by an
unprecedented fall of snow. And as soon as this melted
there came more rain. The peasants were beside themselves, because the sprouting wheat was yellow instead of
green, and many of them had to give back the seeds
distributed by the beet-sugar manufacturers. Both oxen
and tractors risked bogging down if they were taken out,
for the irrigation canals were filled to overflowing and
the fields were one vast sea of mud.

That Tuesday was a market-day, and the arcades
around the square were crowded with peasants and
tenant farmers, condemned to idleness by the bad

weather. Their talk was all of the farm chores which the rain had prevented them from accomplishing, and some of them went so far as to involve the Deity in their tribulations.

'I don't see why Almighty God has it in for us poor farmers!'

As Peppone and Smilzo came out of a café together they caught this exclamation on the wing, and Peppone was quick to turn it to his advantage.

'Almighty God has nothing to do with it, my friends. He's attending to His own business, and there's no use dragging Him in. The fault lies with those people who are exploding the universe.'

Peppone was a natural rabble-rouser. He knew just when to put in a word and had an infallible eye for spotting the one man in the crowd that would make a perfect foil. This time it was Girola, one of the oldest peasants for miles around, who was standing in the front row of the little assembly.

'You there, Girola,' said Peppone, 'in all the ninety-seven years of your life, have you ever seen anything like this crazy weather?'

'No,' said Girola, slowly shaking his head. 'I've seen a bit of everything, storms and floods, and hurricanes that lasted for days or even weeks at a time. But an upset like this, going from one year over to another, is something I've never seen.'

'And what do you say is the cause?' asked Peppone.

'Who knows?' muttered Girola, shrugging his shoulders.

'Don't say that, Girola,' Peppone shouted, warming up to his subject. 'You know, and you've been heard more than once to voice your opinion. There's no reason for you to keep mum about it now. No one's going to claim that it's a fairy-tale, that the rain comes only when God wills it.'

54

So saying Peppone pulled a newspaper out of his pocket.

'Girola's not the only one to have seen clearly; now scientists have reached the same conclusion.'

And Peppone held up the headlines for all to see. No one could say that this was a Party publication; it was an independent newspaper with a Rightist slant.

'Here is the voice of world science,' Peppone continued, 'and it says that we are quite right to be disturbed in our minds over the explosion of the Americans' hydrogen bomb. Their atomic energy has got out of control, and there's no telling what may happen. If you want to read about the damage caused in a three-hundred-mile radius by this last explosion, you can buy the paper. Just to bolster up Girola's opinion, I can tell you this much: a group of Swiss scientists has studied the matter thoroughly and concluded that the earth's balance is threatened by the atomic bomb. Here it is:

'Atomic explosions have created powerful currents in the upper atmosphere, moving in the direction of the North Pole. When the resulting centres of condensation reach the Pole, they are precipitated in the form of snow and ice. Such artificial precipitations may affect the balance of our planet: already the North Pole is eighteen per cent heavier than the South.'

Peppone lifted his head from the paper and looked triumphantly about him. But his satisfaction was marred by the sight of a newcomer to the group, whose presence was anything but welcome. Nevertheless he asked a rhetorical question:

'What is the meaning, then, of this lack of balance between the poles? I never went further than the fifth grade and don't know a word of Latin, so I turn the problem over to an eminent Dutch scientist.

'Dr Schneider, director of the Legerkusen Laboratories in Holland, says that the radio-active particles launched into the atmosphere by atomic explosions act as nuclei of condensation and determine the precipitation of rain and snow.

'So why hold it against Almighty God if we have three feet of snow or a whole year of rain? The Americans are to blame.'

Don Camillo had made his way up to the front row of Peppone's interlocutors, and when Peppone once more lifted his head from the paper, he immediately encountered the priest's eyes. They angered him to the point where he became aggressive.

'Yes,' he repeated. 'Don't hold it against God, hold it against the Americans. Unless the Reverend Father, here present, has such regard for America that he'd rather you took it out on God!'

'No indeed!' exclaimed Don Camillo. 'God has nothing to do with human folly. And He meant men to use their brains to think clearly. We've no business to hold anything against God; let us rather examine ourselves.'

'Father, let's stick to the point,' said Peppone. 'The criminal stupidity of which we are talking is not ours, it's the Americans'. We're speaking of the hydrogen bomb, you know.'

Don Camillo nodded assent.

'Right, Mr Mayor. These things are too serious to be mixed with political propaganda. We must truthfully say that all the disasters, present and future, inherent in experimenting with the atomic bomb are to be laid at the Americans' door. Because, as the mayor has just told us, only the Americans have the bomb.'

Without stopping to think, Peppone retorted:

'Nonsense! The Russians have the bomb too, and in a form a hundred times more powerful. It's no use your trying to twist the facts.'

Don Camillo shook his head mournfully.

'Things are even worse than I thought, Mr Mayor. If it goes on raining, these people will have to be told that the Russians, as well as the Americans, are to blame.'

The little crowd laughed, and Peppone gritted his teeth.

'The Russians are not in the least at fault,' he protested. 'The Americans had the bomb first, and the Russians were forced to develop it for the sake of self-protection.'

Don Camillo threw out his arms in mock despair.

'Mr Mayor, if I were to shoot off my gun, whom would you blame? Me? – or the inventor of gunpowder?'

'And if I were to shoot off a gun at you,' shouted Peppone, 'whose fault would that be? Mine – or that of the bell-ringer at Torricella?'

'Neither one,' said Don Camillo calmly. 'I'd say it was the fault of those who taught you to deny God and shoot at the defenceless clergy.'

'No one has taught me to deny God or shoot at the clergy!' shouted Peppone.

'Then your masters' teaching programme isn't up-to-date. But they'll catch up in time. That's what they've taught everywhere else.'

At this point Smilzo stepped forward.

'Chief, there's one thing we have been taught, and that's not to let an adversary who's in patent bad faith bait us. Don't waste time arguing with him.'

But Peppone was like a dog with a bone, and wouldn't let go. 'We're not to be trapped by professional baiters,' he said, 'but this is an amateur. He deserves a lesson, and we shall see that he gets it.'

Peppone had recovered his aplomb and now he turned to Don Camillo with a smile.

'Father, you say that atomic disasters are due to Americans and Russians alike, because both of them have the bomb. But can you tell me this? Why has public opinion been aroused only now, after the explosion of the

American hydrogen bomb? Why is it that committees of scientists and statesmen have chosen to protest at this particular time? Because we've had ten months of rain and can't sow our beets? Is that it?'

'That I can't say, Mr Mayor.'

'Then I'll tell you. Public opinion and world science have been mobilized for a very good reason. The explosion of the last bomb has proved that atomic energy has escaped the Americans' control. When they set off bombs, nowadays, they don't know what may happen. That's the scientists' opinion, not mine. And who, may I ask, has been clamouring for years for mutual control of atomic energy? Russia or the United States? Russia, Father! America is to blame for having lost control of the atom, while Russia has kept it.'

Don Camillo looked as if he were hard hit by the logic of Peppone. After a pause he said:

'Mr Mayor, I can't say you're altogether wrong. You admit, then, that the American bomb is more powerful than the Russian?'

'I admit nothing of the sort!' shouted Peppone. 'The Russians have the most powerful bomb by far. Only they haven't lost control of it, like the Americans. An effect obtained by calculation and one due to mere chance are two different things altogether.'

Don Camillo nodded his head.

'Mr Mayor, what do you say to continuing the argument with your hands?'

'Hands, feet, machine-guns, cannons, anything you say. . . .'

'Don't misunderstand me; I don't want to get you into a boxing-match. The rain has let up, and we can play a game that may prove to be amusing.'

In the middle of the square there were still some remnants of the carnival: a shooting-gallery, a merry-go-round, and an instrument for measuring a fellow's strength by means of a hammer. The test was to swing a hammer and bring it down on an iron base to which there was attached a measuring-rod and a mobile block which rose, under the blow, to a point numbered between zero and one thousand. If the block went all the way to the top it rang a bell and won a prize. When the two men stood in front of the instrument Don Camillo said:

'I'm the United States, and you're Russia; does that suit you, Mr Mayor?'

The crowd ringed them round and listened in silence.

'The iron block is atomic energy. Is that clear?'

'Yes.'

'I'm America, and since I've lost control of atomic energy I strike at random, not knowing how far I'll go. You're Russia and in full control; you strike a calculated blow.'

Don Camillo took an enormous handkerchief out of his pocket and put it over his eyes.

'I'll just take one last peek in order to see where I'm to place the blow.'

Then Peppone and he each took a hammer.

'Ready?' said Don Camillo.

'Ready,' said Peppone.

Don Camillo spread his legs apart, raised the hammer, and brought it down. The block went up to six hundred.

Peppone struck the next blow and sent it up to seven hundred.

With his second blow Don Camillo sent it up to eight hundred and ten.

Peppone nine hundred.

Don Camillo nine hundred.

Peppone struck wildly and went back to eight hundred and fifty.

'Russia's weakening,' jeered a reactionary at Peppone's shoulder.

And Don Camillo proceeded to score nine hundred and ten. Peppone summoned all his strength, clenched his teeth, and struck a blow that would have shattered an anvil. The iron block went up like a V-2; it passed the thousand mark and hit the electric bell. When he heard the bell ring Don Camillo laid down his hammer and took the handkerchief away from his eyes.

'It happened to you,' he said, 'but it might just as easily have happened to me. Anyhow, now that we've hit the ceiling and made the world go up in flames we may as well go and have a glass of wine together.'

Peppone was perplexed for a moment and then exclaimed:

'No, Father, the comparison doesn't hold water. The fault is yours. If we were to make an agreement to control atomic energy, neither of us would hit the ceiling.'

'Exactly,' said Don Camillo, 'if we knew what the ceiling was. What if it were seven hundred and fifteen or six hundred and three? Do either American or Russian scientists know the limit of Divine Patience?'

It was raining again, and after witnessing the contest, the little crowd had once more taken refuge under the arcades. Don Camillo and Peppone were left alone beside the atomic machine.

'Devil take all bombs!' muttered Don Camillo.

'It's Almighty God's fault for having created Americans and Russians,' said Peppone ill-humouredly.

'Don't be blasphemous, Comrade,' said Don Camillo severely. 'The human race has a big bill to pay, and the present generation has to make up for the deficiencies of the one that preceded it. We're late in coming upon the scene.'

'Then the late-comers are fools,' observed Peppone.

'No, Comrade; the only fools are those that haven't won a good place for themselves in the eternal life to come.'

Peppone pulled the lapels of his coat together and said wryly:

'And while we're waiting for the life to come, it just goes on raining.'

Made in U.S.S.R.

'DON CAMILLO,' said the old Bishop, 'your letter grieved me, not so much for what it said as for what I read between the lines. What is the meaning of your discouragement? Have you lost the faith that has been your bulwark for so long?'

'My faith is unaltered, Your Grace,' said Don Camillo sadly; 'it's a question of technique, of mechanics.'

And when the Bishop looked at him in astonishment he went on to say:

'The young people are getting away from me. It's as if they were racing off on motor-cycles and I were panting after them on foot. It's not faith that's lacking, but a motor-cycle.'

'That's not good reasoning, Don Camillo; it's a play on words.'

'Nevertheless, Your Grace, it reflects the true situation. I don't want to compete with the devil on his own ground; just because young people would rather dance than listen to my sermons, I shan't hold wild parties in the rectory. But because they are so dead set on the films, I want to show some that are a cut above the average. That's the point of what I'm trying to say.'

'How can that be the point, Don Camillo?' said the Bishop, throwing out his arms in bewilderment. 'Haven't you been putting on educational pictures for the last five or six years? What's so new about that?'

'The practice isn't new, Your Grace. And neither is the projector. It's an obsolete model, practically falling to pieces, and . . ."

'That's quite enough, Don Camillo,' the Bishop interrupted. 'If the Good Lord lets obsolete models – such as myself – endure so long, it must be because they're still useful in one way or another. No, Don Camillo, you're trying to trick me. It's not true that you *need* a motorcycle, you just wish you had one!'

But Don Camillo wasn't really trying to trick him. His 16-mm. projector was no longer a machine, it was the ghost of a machine that might have been. And a motorcycle without a front wheel and saddle is a far less serviceable vehicle than shank's pony. Even the best film, when it came out of Don Camillo's projector, was a cinematographic omelette, and the sound-track was a cacophonic zigzag.

'The only thing I can suggest doing,' said the big-city repair-man to whom Don Camillo had taken it, 'is adding it to the rubbish, that is, if the Department of Sanitation will consent to take it!'

When he went back to the village Don Camillo was strongly tempted to throw the thing in the river, but he could not give himself this satisfaction until he was sure of obtaining a replacement, or at least of obtaining the money with which to buy one.

In spite of his remonstrances, the old Bishop did not send Don Camillo away empty-handed. He gave him all the money he could, and although it wasn't very much, Don Camillo went home feeling happy. The first step was taken. There were thousands more steps to go before he reached his goal, but they did not weigh upon him. No landslide ever starts until the first pebble has fallen from the top of the mountain.

And so, after due time, came the promised day, and the arrival of the projector, a brand-new model with a sound-track as smooth as velvet. Don Camillo white-washed the walls of the room and varnished the chairs. He rented a superlative film and posted announcements at every street corner. The afternoon before the great event he ran up and down the streets so often that inevitably he ran into Peppone.

'Is the mayor going to honour us with his presence tonight?' he asked. 'It's such a big occasion that our first citizen should really be on deck.'

'What big occasion do you mean?' asked Peppone in astonishment.

'The opening of the new picture palace.'

'I've never heard of any picture palace, old or new,' answered Peppone. 'All I know is that for some years past you've shown magic-lantern slides for the benefit of choir-boys.'

Don Camillo let this sarcasm go by.

'Let the dead bury their dead,' he suggested. 'We have a real hall and a fabulous new projector.'

'Fabulous as it may be, you're probably coming in on the last guard's van, as usual.'

'After you've been to one of our new shows, you'll see that this guard's van is up at the head of the train and moving faster than even a diesel engine.'

'Fast or slow, the film is a superannuated medium,' said Peppone. 'It's dead as a door-nail, and there's no place for it outside a church hall.'

'What medium is in step with the times, then?' asked Don Camillo. 'The evening class in everyday revolution?'

'Leave politics out of it,' said Peppone. 'Progress has left the film behind. The coming thing is television.'

Just then Smilzo arrived upon the scene and threw out the question:

'Chief, what do you say? The expert is here and wants to know where to put the aerial.'

'Wherever he thinks best. I deal in combustion-engines, and television's not up my street.'

Smilzo hurried away, and after swallowing a lump in his throat, Don Camillo asked:

'Is our mayor a pioneer television owner?'

'Not myself personally, but the workers' Party, whose place is in the vanguard of progress. The TV set is for the People's Palace, and tonight is the first showing. But we shan't offer you any competition, Father. The set is a product of the State Radio Plant of Moscow, and only Party members are invited. I can't ask you to come, Father, much as I regret it, that is, unless you take out a membership card.'

'I admit that I'd like to see what this thing called television is all about,' said Don Camillo between clenched teeth, 'but I can wait a little bit longer.'

'*Fate vobis*,' said Peppone, throwing out his arms.

Don Camillo went home with a queasy feeling in his stomach and took his troubles to the Christ on the main altar.

'Lord,' he panted, 'Peppone and his gang have a TV set!'

'They're not the only ones in the world, are they?' Christ answered. 'And it's not a death-dealing machine, is it?'

'They're not the only ones in the world, but they're the only ones in the village.'

'But why do you worry? Are you afraid that the appeal of something so new may lure some of your followers into the bear's lair?'

'No, only Party members can enjoy it. But I had hoped that my film hall would attract some of Peppone's hangers-on, and I could save them from the bear's embraces.'

Christ sighed.

'Are these your weapons, Don Camillo?' he asked. 'I didn't have any machines with which to seize men from the devil's grasp and put them on the path of righteousness.'

'Lord, forgive me,' said Don Camillo, humbly bowing his head. 'But the devil didn't have any machines then, either. If the devil rides a motor-cycle, why should I pursue him on foot?'

'Don Camillo, I can't follow your cycling metaphor. But the vehicles that carry men to heaven or hell are just the same now as they were then.'

The television set poisoned Don Camillo's entire evening, and in spite of the success of the film show, he was unable to sleep. Something about the affair was not clear in his mind, and the thought of this elusive, shadowy zone would not let him rest. The next morning, when he looked out of the window that gave on to the church square and saw the television aerial rising above the People's Palace, he was suddenly enlightened. That afternoon he managed to run into Peppone again and said to him brusquely:

'In this television business, are you following a directive from the higher echelons, or did you think it up yourself?'

'What do directives have to do with television?' asked Peppone. 'I do what I please.'

'Then you're a jackass, Peppone. Only a jackass could imagine that anyone in this village would take out membership in the Communist Party for the sake of seeing the idiocies projected by your teletrap, "made in U.S.S.R.". Who believes that they have television sets in Russia?'

'Oh, I forgot that in Russia they don't have either watches or bicycles!' said Peppone, throwing out his arms. 'According to you, this set of ours, which has "made in U.S.S.R." on every single part, is really a "product of U.S.A.", is that it? As you like! Those that have television can enjoy it, and the have-nots will just have to swallow their bile!'

Don Camillo's anger was plain to see, and he did well to go away without answering this last sally. When he reached the rectory he had to hear some first-hand reports on the village reaction to the new TV.

'It seems to be positively wonderful.'

'And it was really made in Russia, so they say.'

'The Reds who went to the first showing are wild with joy. They say the Americans had better go and bury their heads in the sand.'

That night Don Camillo turned over and over in his bed, and his long quest for sleep was thwarted by the chatter of several noise-makers who wagged their tongues immediately under his window, on the church square.

'Too bad, though, that when they have colour TV we'll need a new set.'

'A new set? Not a bit of it! They haven't got colour at all in America, but in Russia they've had it for the last two years. And the sets made for export are geared to both black-and-white and colour. Did you see that red lever on the right side? You just pull it down, and there's the whole rainbow.'

'If I were Peppone, I'd put it on display at the Party's retail store, so that everybody could see. That way they'd stop saying that we keep it to ourselves because it's either home-grown or made in America.'

'Not on your life! They can say what they like, but if they want to see, they'll have to join the Party!'

Don Camillo was a captive audience. And when they stopped talking so loudly and began to laugh and whisper, he jumped out of bed and glued his ear to the aperture of the shutters.

'. . . a hall just as dismal as the other . . .'

'. . . films more idiotic than ever . . .'

'. . . and they say the sound is ear-splitting . . .'

'. . . but what should he know about machines? They saw him coming . . .'

'. . . you know what it is, when a man has a wad of money, whether it's a few liras more or less . . .'

In order not to burst with rage, Don Camillo dived back into bed, where he didn't shut an eye before morning. But by the time morning came he had swallowed his anger and his brain was functioning in a normal manner. 'A canny player plays his cards close to the chest, and no one can guess what he has up his sleeve. If you're not showing your Soviet TV set, it's because the whole thing's a big story. You'll puncture your own balloon, if I give you time, Comrade Peppone!'

And so Don Camillo inaugurated a policy of complete indifference. When anyone spoke of the famous Russian TV set, he answered with a smile:

'If the Russians have the atomic bomb, why shouldn't they have TV sets and send them to their friends abroad?'

'What about the colour TV?'

'They've always been colourful! Why shouldn't they apply this quality to television?'

And so one, two, three months went by. Every evening there was a change of the guard at the People's Palace, and a different group went to see the show, gathering afterwards below Don Camillo's window, on the church square, for an exchange of extravagantly laudatory impressions. Don Camillo was rudely awakened, and had to listen in grim silence. He held out for some time, but on perhaps the ninetieth occurrence it was too much for him to endure. 'Enough is enough!' he muttered to himself. 'I've taken all I can, God forgive me!'

This was ten days after the snowstorm which had caused the collapse of the roof of the People's Palace and the attic below. The roof and the attic ceiling had been promptly repaired, but the night watchman's quarters were still uninhabitable, because the walls had been soaked with water and the cement was not yet dry enough to permit removal of the scaffolding. The watchman, Lungo, and his wife and child were temporarily quartered elsewhere, and from midnight to four o'clock in the morning the People's Palace was empty.

One foggy evening a man went through the open door leading to the courtyard and climbed resolutely to the attic, where he lay for several hours in ambush. At midnight Lungo let down the iron curtain at the front of the retail store, gathered up the day's receipts and accounts, inspected the premises, locked the doors, and went to his mother-in-law's house. The intruder had such self-control that he waited two hours more before going into action. Slowly he made his way to the ground floor and the assembly hall. All the shutters were closed, and he was assured of complete privacy. With the aid of a torch he surveyed the scene. What he was looking for seemed to be veiled by a piece of cloth at the opposite end of the room. He walked over, removed the cloth, and gazed upon a shiny, new TV set, surmounted by a metal plate bearing the inscription 'Made in U.S.S.R.'. It wouldn't have been very hard to nail a plate of this kind on to a case containing an American or British or Italian machine, and so the investigator detached the back cover. At this point his emotion was so great that he dropped the torch on to the floor.

'Lord,' panted Don Camillo, throwing himself on to his knees before the altar, 'something utterly astounding has happened. A fellow who accidentally got into the People's Palace last night took a look at the famous Russian TV set. And what do you think was inside the case? Nothing! Did you hear me? N-o-t-h-i-n-g! The case was empty!' And after wiping the perspiration from his brow he went on: 'Yes, Lord, empty! For ninety consecutive evenings those poor fools have taken turns going in groups to the People's Palace and then coming out to tell of the miraculous things they've seen. What colossal nerve, Lord! For three months no one has let the cat out of the bag. Just imagine the fun there'll be tomorrow, when the secret is known! The Russian TV! And yet I'll wager that if the discoverer doesn't tell his story they're quite capable of keeping up the farce indefinitely. Isn't it utterly ridiculous? Are they stark mad, to play a part like this, without ever giving themselves away? Self-discipline, they call it, but I have another name . . . Lord, you aren't even listening. . . .'

'I was thinking of the sorrows of the world, Don Camillo, not of the tall tales you've been telling. What is it, then, that the visitor to the People's Palace saw?'

'Lord, a fellow accidentally got in there last night and saw the famous TV set,' said Don Camillo, hanging his head. 'It's authentically "made in U.S.S.R.".'

Don Camillo didn't breathe a word to a soul, but a week later when he ran into Peppone he couldn't resist remarking:

'Comrade, when will your faithful give up the game of the empty box?'

'When the time is ripe, Rev.!'

'Isn't it all very silly?'

'Just try getting up something equally silly among your highly respectable people!'

To this Don Camillo found no reply.

The next morning the village was startled by an amazing piece of news. A short circuit had caused the famous TV set to go up in flames.

'*But the enemies of the People have no cause to rejoice,*' said the poster which Peppone put up on the façade of the People's Palace. '*The working-class, no matter how ground down it may be, will have another T.V!*'

They took up a collection, and ten days later the People's Palace no longer had an empty box; it had a box full of TV.

'It's not nearly as good as the Russian set we had before,' proclaimed Peppone's henchmen, 'but it's better than nothing.'

And from their point of view, they weren't so very wrong.

Inflation in the Po Valley

THE question of television continued to be a sore point
with Don Camillo, and smart salesmen have a way of
sensing such things. The young man with the handsome
tan brief-case was all smiles when he came to the rectory,
insisting that all he wanted was to make the acquaintance
of the most famous priest of the lower Po valley. Don
Camillo still had some hundred jars of 'Atomic Floor
Wax' in the basement, and he wasn't going to fall for
sales talk, no matter how many blandishments went with
it.

'Thanks for your kind words, but I really don't need
a thing.'

'Father, you misunderstand me,' the young man protested. 'I'm no salesman, I work for Guardian . . .'

'I see, it's life insurance . . .'

'No, Father, you must be thinking of some other
organization. Guardian Purchases is an entirely different
matter, as you can see for yourself.'

These last words meant that he had managed to open

his brief-case and put a dazzlingly illustrated catalogue into Don Camillo's hands.

'Motor-cycles, bicycles, cameras, typewriters, refrigerators, radio and television sets . . . Guardian buys all these things direct from the makers at such a discount that it can make house-to-house sales on the instalment plan, with no increase over the list prices.'

Don Camillo tried to give back the catalogue, but the young man would have none of it.

'Don't worry, Father, I'm not here to sell. I only mean to give you an idea of all the lines we carry. If ever you want to buy any of these things, I'm sure you'll come to us. For instance, some day you'll surely get a television set, and it'll be worth your while to look over our large assortment. . . .'

The smiling salesman must have been Satan in disguise, or else how could he have known that Don Camillo was crazy to have a television set? But so far nothing serious had happened. Just to look at photographs of television sets didn't mean promising to buy one. The young man made this very clear.

'You have here an enormous range of models, from the cheapest to the most luxurious, all of them well-known makes. You can see for yourself that we charge the normal retail price, and the payments are extra-ordinarily easy. We call ourselves "Guardian Purchases" because our system actually guards and protects you. The debt you contract with us practically pays itself.'

Don Camillo was so taken with the television sets that he forgot about the store of useless wax in the basement. But he did not forget that his personal finances were disastrously low. And so, after feasting his eyes on the catalogue, he insisted on returning it.

'I'll keep what you told me in mind,' he said by way of farewell.

'Thank you,' said the salesman, tucking it away in his brief-case. 'Just let me repeat that you needn't worry about the money. The day you decide to make your purchase just let me know and I'll come to write out the contract and pick up the initial payment. Of course, if here and now you happen to have as little as five thousand liras, it would be even simpler. . . .'

He must indeed have been Satan in disguise, or else how could he have known that, besides the burning desire for a television set, Don Camillo had exactly five thousand liras in his wallet? In any case, when he walked out of the rectory he had them in his pocket, together with a signed contract and a sheaf of signed promissory notes. Of course, he said that these notes were a mere formality and Don Camillo mustn't worry about meeting them. Don Camillo didn't worry. For some time he had warm feelings about the smiling young man, because the television set was a beauty and worked very well. But one day he found himself in trouble.

At the end of the fourth month Don Camillo couldn't meet the payment. The television set was his own personal luxury and he had to pay for it out of his own personal funds, which at this point were not merely low but virtually non-existent. Eighteen thousand liras aren't so very much, but if a poor country priest hasn't got them, what is he to do? He can't work overtime or give private instruction in the catechism. There was no excuse for appealing to his wealthier parishioners, for no object or institution of charity was involved. And no matter how poor he was, Don Camillo had his dignity. He couldn't borrow money to meet the payment due for a television set; after all, it was an extravagance and he ought never to have taken it if he didn't have extra means.

Finally he wrote to Guardian Purchases, but they wrote back that although they appreciated the unusual circumstances in which he found himself and were truly sorry, there was nothing they could do. The note had been sent to the bank and he must either pay up or submit to the bank's demand for payment. Complications increased, because Don Camillo was unable to pay the next instalment either. This time he did not have the nerve to write; he simply said a prayer and waited for pandemonium to break loose. The situation was particularly delicate for this reason. Although with time Don Camillo would doubtless have been able to restore his affairs to good order, a local election was at hand, and this was not the moment to have the bank publish his name. Don Camillo was not a candidate for office; he was not even enrolled in any political party. But the Christian Democrats' opponents were sure to seize any pretext for attacking a priest. Furthermore, to tell the truth, Don Camillo had been active in the last national election and the Christian Democrats had discussed their tactics with him. He broke out into cold perspiration at the thought of what Peppone and his gang would do if they had the bank's list of bad accounts in their hands.

After a number of sleepless nights and tormented days, the time for the bank bulletin's publication came round, and Don Camillo went all the way to the city to get a copy. Sure enough, the first thing he saw was his own name. He went back to the village in a state of great dismay and shut himself up in the rectory where nobody could see him. For he imagined that everyone must be in the know. That evening he ate no supper and could not even make up his mind to go to bed, but paced up and down the hall, with black thoughts crowding his mind. Peppone and his gang had acquired a formidable weapon against him, and he could just hear the accusations they would make in political meetings. His horror was all the more intense because he seemed to hear the crowd laughing. He must do something – anything – about it. And so, abruptly, he did.

Peppone was still hammering away in his workshop, and the sight of Don Camillo caused him to start.

'You must have something on your conscience,' said Don Camillo.

'A priest flitting about by night is bound to startle even an honest man,' said Peppone dryly. 'What do you want?'

There was no use making a short story long.

'I want to talk with you, man to man.'

'What about?'

'The promissory notes.'

Peppone threw his hammer into one corner.

'I have something to say, man to man, too,' he said. 'And I'd like to point out that, in spite of our enmity, I've never made political capital out of your personal misfortunes.'

'I can say the same thing,' said Don Camillo.

'I'm not so sure about that,' Peppone grumbled. 'But there's one thing that *is* sure: if you dare to be funny about my overdue note, I'll wring your neck.'

Don Camillo thought he must have misunderstood.

'What's your note got to do with it?' he asked.

Out of his pocket Peppone pulled a crumpled paper, which he thrust roughly at the priest.

'If you haven't seen or heard about it, you'll be sure to see or hear tomorrow. On the list of notes that have not been honoured there's one signed by your humble servant, Giuseppe Bottazzi.'

And there, under the letter *B*, was listed a note for twenty thousand liras in Peppone's name. Don Camillo had never noticed it simply because he was so intent upon looking for his own.

'Is that the only thing of interest you found?' he asked, shaking the bulletin in front of Peppone's nose.

'I confine myself to my own business,' said Peppone. 'I wanted to know if I was there, and there I was.'

Don Camillo put the bulletin into his hand, pointing to a certain line. Peppone read and re-read it, and then stared hard at Don Camillo.

'No!'

'Yes!' Don Camillo exclaimed. 'Devil take "Guardian Purchases"!'

Peppone started.

'"Guardian Purchases"? A most agreeable young fellow with a big tan brief-case?'

'Exactly.'

'And did you get a refrigerator, too?'

'No, a television set.'

Peppone launched into a tirade against instalment buying, an institution worse than the atomic bomb. Just a spot of cash and a trifle to pay every month, a debt that pays itself. . . . Then when you're unable to pay, you see that you were the trifler, and two hundred thousand liras of debt are . . . two hundred thousand liras. Finally he calmed down.

'Well, since my refrigerator is working perfectly well, and you're in the same boat, there'll be no political consequences. Why worry? Don't you agree?'

'That's what I say,' said Don Camillo. Then a sudden thought caused him to turn pale.

'What about the third ticket?' he shouted.

The third ticket was a group of candidates put up by the Rightists, who were opposing both Peppone's Reds and the Christian Democrats' Shield and Cross. These candidates would have a cogent argument against both their adversaries, and the village would enjoy no end of laughter. Pietro Follini, the Rightist leader, was a fast thinker and an eloquent speaker. Peppone too turned pale.

'The idea that because of these filthy notes they may bracket me with the wearer of a clerical collar makes me see red!' he shouted.

'And the idea of being dragged down to the level of a godless fool makes me see black!' retorted Don Camillo.

They mulled it over for a quarter of an hour, and then Peppone pulled on his jacket and said:

'I'll go through the fields, and you go along the river. We'll have a showdown with that miserable Pietro Follini. First, you try to make him see reason. If he doesn't respond, I'll make him see stars.'

Follini had gone to bed, but he came downstairs when he heard Don Camillo calling. Great was his amazement when he saw Peppone beside him.

'Have you set up a common front?' he asked. 'I'm not surprised. Reds and clericals have the same end in view: dictatorship!'

'Follini, keep your wit for political meetings,' said Peppone. 'See if you can grasp what Don Camillo is going to tell you.'

They went to sit down in the parlour, and Don Camillo at once showed Follini the bank bulletin.

'Have you seen that?' he asked.

'Yes, I've seen it. I went to the city this morning for the express purpose of buying it. When I saw my name, I took it hard. But when I saw the names of the priest and the mayor, I felt better.'

Don Camillo took back the bulletin and thumbed nervously through it. Under the *F*'s there was Pietro Follini, listed as owing forty thousand liras. The three men looked at one another in silence, until Don Camillo said:

'I owe Guardian Purchases twenty thousand liras for a television set; he owes them the same for a refrigerator. How about you?'

'I owe them forty thousand for a television set *and* a refrigerator. Both of them are working very well.'

'Same here!' said Peppone.

'Same here!' echoed Don Camillo.

Follini opened a bottle of wine. They drank together and before Don Camillo went back along the river he muttered:

'I'm glad there's not a fourth ticket!'

And before Peppone went back through the fields he mumbled:

'We're neatly matched. Television against television, refrigerator against refrigerator, and promissory note against promissory note! It's democracy in action!'

The Devil Swishes His Tail

MICHAELMAS was close at hand, and festive preparations were under way, when the bombshell burst. It burst in the form of a notice posted by Don Camillo.

For too many years the coming holiday has been celebrated with indecent public dancing in the square. It is time for all good Christians to join in outlawing this immoral spectacle. If foolish folk of both sexes and all ages must cavort like monkeys to the accompaniment of jungle cacophony, let them find a place more appropriate to their carnival than the square in front of God's house.

It is prohibited by law to organize public dancing or other offensive activities in the neighbourhood of a church, and I call upon the duly constituted authorities to enforce this prohibition.

Of course, the notice sent Peppone into a paroxysm of anger, for he and his gang were the sponsors of the 'indecent public dancing' in question. The 'Public Welfare Committee' was called into immediate session at the People's Palace, and proceeded to discuss countermeasures to this act of clerical aggression. When Brusco was called upon to speak, he declared:

'We have all the time in the world to counter-attack. Just now we must concentrate on obtaining a permit for the dancing. After that is cleared, the priest can protest till he's blue in the face.'

The majority seconded him, and Peppone went by bicycle to police headquarters.

'I was just about to bring you the permit,' the sergeant told him.

'So we can go ahead with our dancing, just as in previous years?' asked Peppone with relief.

'Yes, you have the all-clear of the provincial police. Only you mustn't dance in the square. The carnival ground isn't the legal distance from the church.'

'But, Sergeant,' Peppone exclaimed, turning purple with rage, 'the distance was legal enough for the past seven years! What's the matter with it now?'

'The distance was never legal, Mr Mayor. But as long as the priest didn't kick, the police winked at it. Now that there's been a protest, we've had to open our eyes. It's a matter of only a few yards, and it's up to the priest's discretion.'

'But if we can't dance in the square, where *can* we dance?' asked Peppone in dismay.

'Anywhere you like, just as long as the carnival is set up at a legal distance from the church. The permit is issued under that condition.'

Peppone called the committee together again and explained the situation.

'This cursed village seems to be laid out in a way designed to benefit the clergy and poison honest working people! If you take away the square, there's no space large enough to hold a carnival. It's either the square, or the outskirts; there's no other alternative. And if you stage it in the outskirts, what happens? First, you miss the crowd from the cafés and taverns on the square; second, you have to pay rent for the use of the land; and third, you are humiliated by having to operate in the middle of a sea of mud, littered with fallen apples.'

Brusco had a word to put in.

'Chief,' he said, 'since the sergeant told you it was up to the priest's discretion, why don't we go and talk reason to Don Camillo?'

Peppone pounded the table with his fist.

'I'll never lower myself to the level of a priest! Never!'

'I didn't say you should be the one to go parley with him. There are twelve of us, all able to speak up and hold our own. Let's write our names on slips of paper and then draw one out of a hat. Tell the barman's son to bring us something to write on.'

And so, after each one had written his name, folded his sheet of paper, and thrown it into Brusco's hat, the barman's son proceeded to the drawing.

'Peppone!' he announced.

'Did it have to be me?' Peppone groaned.

Brusco threw out his arms.

'Never mind; I'll go,' muttered Peppone. 'Brusco, you stay here, and the rest of you can go on home.'

When Brusco and he were alone together, Peppone picked up the hat and took out the eleven remaining ballots. He unfolded them, one by one, and spread them out in a row on the table.

'Look at those, Brusco, and then tell me whether or not you're a bunch of rascals!'

Brusco examined the ballots and saw that every one bore the name of Peppone.

'Brusco,' Peppone shouted again, seizing his companion by the shoulder; 'is this the way the comrades rat on their leader?'

'No, Chief, it only goes to show what confidence they have in him!'

'Father,' said Peppone, sitting down on the chair which Don Camillo pointed out to him, 'have we come to the point where we have to argue over a matter of inches?'

'I'm not arguing over inches,' Don Camillo replied. 'I'm raising a moral question, which defies all measurement.'

'But in past years you didn't raise any moral question. There wasn't anything wrong then, so what can there be now?'

'There was always a moral question involved, Mr Mayor. But I was hoping you would see it for yourself.'

'It's much simpler than that,' jeered Peppone. 'The fact is that you were more afraid of us in past years.'

'I was never afraid of a living soul, and you know it,' said Don Camillo, shaking his head. 'If I didn't step in before, it's just because I knew people were incapable of seeing the light. It's no use arguing with madmen. Now the atmosphere is calmer, and the question can be raised. When people have lost all sense of proportion there's no point in talking about inches. Everything has its proper time.'

'I see, Father,' assented Peppone. 'According to you, the Communists have lost strength and so you can speak your mind. You may think as you please, but I consider you're making a mistake. One day you'll find out that the Communists still count.'

'I don't doubt it, Comrade; otherwise I should have ceased to combat them. Wolves stay wolves, and sheep can't be anything but sheep. When the wolves are prowling around the sheepfold, the sheep daren't stick out their noses, but when the wolves go back to the woods, the sheep may come out and nibble a few blades of grass.'

'So I'm a wolf, am I?' muttered Peppone.

'Yes.'

'And you're an innocent lamb, is that it?'

'Exactly.'

'A fine lamb you are!' shouted Peppone, leaping to his feet. 'You're a Bengal tiger!'

As he went towards the door, Don Camillo called out: 'See you soon, baboon!'

Peppone, still fuming, informed the committee of the upshot of this conversation.

'Curse that priest! Devil take him and his legal distance! We'll dance in the outskirts, but with two orchestras playing so loudly that they'll be heard on the square. It's only a matter of finding the right location.'

While Peppone was holding a meeting in the People's Palace, Don Camillo addressed a group of landowners whose property lay in the outskirts of the village.

'I called you together,' he said, 'because you are good Christians and hence lovers of law and order. Once more the day sacred to Saint Michael is going to be defiled by the Reds' public ball. I have managed to prevent its being held, quite shamelessly, on the square. But the Reds won't give up so easily; they'll simply transfer it to the outskirts. Even there, they'll be checkmated, because you'll refuse them the use of your land. I trust you are all in agreement.'

His eight hearers were all ferociously anti-Red, but Don Camillo's words were not greeted with the enthusiasm which he had expected. They said nothing, and stared at the mat on the oval table before them.

'Well, then?' said Don Camillo in amazement. 'If you don't see things in the same light, just say so.'

They stared at one another, until finally Cerelli said what was on all their minds.

'Father, you're quite right. But to tell the truth, I don't see the necessity for a clash with the Communists on this particular occasion. If they ask me for the use of a piece of land and are willing to pay for it, why should I say no?'

The other seven admitted that they felt the same way. Don Camillo crossed his arms over his capacious chest.

'Very well. Your priest calls for your help and you refuse to give it.'

'No,' said Cerelli. 'We'd do anything for you, Father. But you mustn't ask us to do more than we feel like doing.'

'And what if I were to ask you to do something involving no risk and giving you a chance to make some money?' asked Don Camillo, bringing his fist down on the table. 'How would you feel about that?'

'It sounds good, Father.'

'Splendid! How much do you think Peppone may offer you for your land?'

They said somewhere between fifteen and twenty thousand liras.

'Excellent,' said Don Camillo. 'Then the eight of you must agree that anyone who wants your land must put down a sixty-thousand lira deposit. Just think, some one of you may actually pocket that much money!'

This idea won his listeners' favour.

'Good,' said Don Camillo. 'But we'll have to be sure that no one puts anything over on his neighbours by accepting less. Are you willing to give me your word of honour that nothing less than a deposit of sixty thousand liras will induce you to do business?'

They all swore, and shook hands on it. It's not that way in the city, but in the Po valley, when a man gives his word it is considered binding. And so Don Camillo went to bed with his mind at rest. To spend sixty thousand liras for a couple of days would be utter folly, and Peppone's plans were doomed from the start. It wasn't really the season for a carnival, anyhow; the bulk of the dancers would come from other villages near by. Without the usual contributions from the storekeepers on the square and faced with the prospect of digging up sixty thousand liras in cash, Peppone would have to surrender.

Peppone knew nothing of the trouble which Don Camillo was brewing for him, and the next day he sent Smilzo out on a reconnoitring mission.

'Go and see about renting some land. Remember that you are fortunate enough to be dealing with eight separate owners. If any one of them asks too much money, you can afford to pass him by in favour of one of the seven others. Don't worry about their doing you in. Rich people don't know how to organize such a thing as joint action. Their only wish is to rub up against one another. So remember that I don't want to spend more than twelve thousand liras, to be paid when the carnival is over.'

Smilzo went bravely off, and when the first landowner he approached asked for sixty thousand liras cash, he laughed in his face. He laughed again when the second made the same demand. But the third aroused no more than a faint smile, and the fourth wiped that off his face. When he had finished making the rounds, Smilzo came gloomily back to where he had started.

'Chief,' he began, 'two hours ago you said that rich people were too stupid to organize a joint action.'

'Well, what of it?' asked Peppone.

'You're dead wrong, Chief. This time they've all banded together and none of them will rent his land for less than sixty thousand liras, paid in advance.'

Peppone began to describe in a loud voice that sink of iniquity which was the soul of Don Camillo. He concluded his tirade by saying:

'Comrades, there are two alternatives before us: either to concede the clericals' victory, or to squeeze out sixty thousand liras. Choose! But think first which course is the more expensive in the long run.'

'Chief, we haven't really an idea of the market prices,' Brusco observed.

'But you have an Ideal, for which you are willing to die, haven't you?' Peppone shouted.

Brusco wanted to answer that pledging one's life to an Ideal and promising to pay sixty thousand liras are two quite different things. Especially when the liras have to be put down on the spot, for a man who pledges his life to an Ideal isn't compelled to die in advance for it. But he did not say any of these things, and so it was decided that a clerical victory would cost more grief than the outlay of sixty thousand liras. Because none of the Committee had brought any money, Peppone was the one to fork out.

Don Camillo took it hard when he learned that Peppone had put down sixty thousand liras in cash for the rent of a field to the left of the Molinetto road, just outside the village. He hadn't anticipated any such blow. And when he read posted announcements of the carnival, he took it even harder. The posters made extravagant promises: prizes for the best single dancers, the best-matched and most ill-assorted couples, and the presence of two orchestras, together with well-known popular singers.

'They're getting up something tremendous,' his informants told Don Camillo. 'It's advertised in the villages for miles around, with a special appeal to their Party groups. Yes, it's become a political football, an act of resistance to clerical interference.'

Don Camillo lost his head. Wasn't the whole fault his? Hadn't he asked for trouble? If he hadn't intervened, the carnival tents would have been pitched on the square; Peppone and his gang would have organized the usual uninspired celebration.

Yes, Don Camillo lost his head. Whenever this happened the consequences were disastrous, for the devil's tail began to swish with anticipation. After having foamed impotently at the mouth with anger, one whole day long, Don Camillo called his most reliable follower, Gigi Lollini.

'Gigi,' Don Camillo said to the young man, 'have you seen what those damned souls are up to now?'

'Yes, Father, I have.'

'Gigi, we've got to make it fail. You must form a committee and set up another carnival, just across the way. If the Reds have two orchestras, then hire three; if they have three contests, stage half a dozen. You have a head start, because while Peppone's had to advance sixty thousand liras, you'll get the land for next to nothing. Go to Cerelli, whose place is just opposite the one rented by Peppone. Only don't let on that I'm in any way concerned. A parish priest can't sponsor a forty-eight-hour dance marathon.'

Lollini was a violent anti-Red and undertook the assignment with enthusiasm. He scuttled away and went first to rent some of Cerelli's land. Soon he came back to the rectory.

'Father, that old skinflint wants sixty thousand liras. I asked the other six, and they told me that they had all promised to accept no less. After imposing these terms on Peppone, they feel they must stick to their guns. The main thing is that they don't want trouble. . . . I found some fellows to go into partnership with me, but they refuse to spend more than fifteen thousand liras, and I haven't any cash to advance myself.'

Yes, the devil's tail was swishing ominously. Don Camillo paced up and down the rectory hall and then said:

'I can get my motor-cycle later on. Here are the sixty-five thousand liras I've been saving up; I'll give you all but five of them.'

'Don't worry, Father, you'll get them all back. We have a programme that will put the Reds to shame, and we'll give it plenty of publicity. . . .'

The next day the village was filled with posters announcing 'the carnival of the century', put on by the 'Good Fun Company'. Afternoon and evening dancing were to appropriately honour the feast of Saint Michael.

The morning of the last day before the celebration Smilzo and Lollini came to blows over trifles. Soon after noon a truck arrived with material for the Reds' carnival, and two hours later, while it was still being erected, came the material for Don Camillo's, just across the way. At two-thirty, the rival gangs met in the middle of the road and beat each other up enthusiastically. By evening, both carnivals were nearly ready, but it looked as if the next day were going to be the saddest Michaelmas the village had ever known.

'Lord,' said Don Camillo to the crucified Christ on the main altar, 'if You don't step in, tomorrow is going to be ugly for all of us. Everything in this crazy village revolves round politics, even an immoral but non-political ball. Because of the rivalry between the two groups which have organized the dances, it's likely that the celebration will end in a free-for-all fight. Unfortunately, a minister of your church is mixed up in it, because he ill-advisedly supported one group against the other. He had good intentions, Lord. . . .'

'Don Camillo!' the Lord interrupted, 'you know what's paved with good intentions! And since when does the end justify the means?'

'Lord,' whispered Don Camillo, 'unless it's a lie circulated by God's enemies, You Yourself once drove the money-changers from the temple. Of course, I don't say that beating people up is a sin, but after all . . .'

'Don Camillo, how do you dare criticize your own God?'

'I'm not sacrilegious, Lord, but I do say that when one of God's creatures has an ailing tooth, then even if the dentist hurts him by pulling it out . . .'

'Don Camillo,' Christ said gravely: 'why do you walk in the tortuous path of sophistry?'

'Because I've got off the right track, Lord, and I wish someone would put me straight, with a swift kick, if need be.'

Slowly Don Camillo raised his head to look at Christ's face, but his eyes remained on the feet, nailed to the Cross.

It was a terrible night for Don Camillo. He woke up at four o'clock and ran to the window. It was raining, raining buckets and torrents. And as the hours went by, it continued to rain. It rained all day, and by midnight the floor-boards of the two carnivals were floating in mud. It rained all of three days more, and amid the downpour both carnivals were dismantled and shipped away. Then, when God willed it, out came the sun, and Don Camillo ran into Peppone.

'Father,' Peppone said bitterly, 'your manoeuvres cost me sixty thousand liras out of my own pocket.'

'They cost me the same,' sighed Don Camillo.

'That makes me feel better,' said Peppone.

'Then we're even,' put in the priest.

'But on Michaelmas of next year . . .' Peppone began, threateningly.

'You mean, if it isn't raining . . .'

'I forgot that you clericals are in on God's little secrets,' Peppone shouted angrily. 'But it won't go on like this forever. There'll be a day of reckoning!'

'That is, if it doesn't rain, Mr Mayor!'

'We'll fight with umbrellas,' Peppone said solemnly, as if he were speaking for history.

And in order not to spoil the effect, Don Camillo said nothing more.

Ring out the Old, Ring in the New

DON CAMILLO was called to the Bishopric, but since the old Bishop was ill Monsignor Contini received him.

'Tell me all about the "Bridge" church.'

This was the last question Don Camillo had expected and for a moment he was so taken aback that he could not open his mouth.

'The "Bridge" church? Forgive me, Monsignore, but I don't know what you mean.'

'It's not so hard to grasp. There's a building within the boundaries of your parish known as the "Bridge" church, isn't there?'

'Yes, Monsignore.'

'Well then, tell me all about it.'

Don Camillo gathered his thoughts together and then told the brief story.

'The so-called "Bridge" church was until fifty years ago in an independent parish in the Pioppetta section. Then, as the village grew, the Pioppetta parish was integrated with ours. But the "Bridge" church remained officially open, by virtue of a yearly mass celebrated on St Michael's day.'

Monsignor Contini shook his head.

'According to what I'm told, there's something more to say. The faithful who live out that way would be happy if mass were said there every Sunday. Isn't it so?'

'Undoubtedly, Monsignore. The Pioppetta section is quite far out, and the road leading to the centre of the village is in miserable condition. To come in every Sunday is a real hardship, especially for the old people.'

'Then everything we have been told is true. We are distressed only that you shouldn't have been the one to inform us.'

'But, Monsignore, no one from the Pioppetta section has ever said anything to me.'

'Very well. But when you've noticed a number of people from there failing to turn up at Sunday mass, especially during the winter, you might have thought to report the situation. In any case, now that it has been reported, we shall see that something is done about it. Every Sunday and holy day of obligation mass shall be said at the "Bridge" church.'

Don Camillo bowed his head.

'With God's help, I shall carry out the Bishop's orders.'

'With God's help and the help of the young priest we are going to send to assist you. We aren't asking you to make an unreasonable effort.'

Don Camillo's mouth fell open.

'But, I really don't need . . .' he stammered.

'Don Camillo,' Monsignor Contini interrupted him, 'we know your good will. But for all of us the years are going by. You're getting to be, well, shall we say, a mature man. . . .'

'I?' exclaimed Don Camillo, throwing out his chest. 'I can still carry a three-hundred weight sack of wheat up to a second storey!'

'I don't doubt it! But your job is not weight-lifting, and muscles are not the prime requisites.'

'Monsignore, I've always carried out my priestly mission. . . .'

'I'm sure of that, Don Camillo. But we can't expect you to go beyond the call of duty. We shall send you a bright, enthusiastic young fellow, who'll relieve you of some of the drudgery of parish work. The rectory is big enough to lodge him, and the generosity of Divine Providence is unfailing, so that you'll have no trouble in putting him up.'

'I shall obey orders, as faithfully as ever.'

'As *almost* ever,' his superior corrected him. 'We know Don Camillo and esteem him at his just worth, but in all truth we can't say that he is an example of perfect discipline. Don Camillo is an honest, diligent priest, but he has a bit of temperament . . . or am I mistaken?'

'No, Monsignore. I admit to my weaknesses.'

'Let's forget about them,' said Monsignor Contini. 'When you go back to the village, put the "Bridge" church in order, so that it can be turned to full-time use as soon as possible.'

'Monsignore,' said Don Camillo, throwing out his arms. 'When it was a matter of saying only one mass a year, I brought the necessary supplies with me. But what are we to do now? The church is an empty shell.'

'There are people in your village who are not only well off, but who have means far beyond their needs. You must make the rounds of all those who are in a position to give. Tell them that by contributing to this little church they will warm their ailing Bishop's heart.'

These words particularly caught Don Camillo's attention.

'Is he so very ill, Monsignore?'

'Yes, but there's no reason to be alarmed or to spread the alarm. It's nothing you can put your finger on, but simply the effect of old age. What His Grace needs above all is complete rest and peace of mind. We must not allow him to worry.'

'He needn't worry about the little church under my jurisdiction!' exclaimed Don Camillo. 'All that he wishes shall be done. Even if I have to use brute force . . .'

'Come, come, Don Camillo! . . .'

'That's just a manner of speaking.'

The 'Bridge' church was in a sorry state. The walls were sturdy enough, but the ceiling looked like a sieve; the plaster was in tatters, the floor uneven, and the pews cracked or cracking. Even a minimum amount of repairs called for a considerable sum of money, and the collection of such a sum called, in turn, for what seemed like an infinity of patient endeavour. When Don Camillo had drawn up an estimate of the costs, he drew a deep breath as well. 'I'll do everything I can, and Divine Providence will look after the rest,' he concluded.

His campaign got off to a lame start, when he knocked first at the door of Filotti, the richest landowner in the vicinity. Don Camillo spoke of the old Bishop and of the pleasure it would give him to hear that the little 'Bridge' church was back in use. But Filotti shook his head.

'Father, when you've asked for money for the poor or for the Orphan Asylum, I've always been happy to contribute. But this time I don't feel like giving. The village church is quite sufficient. And, frankly, I don't see why, at this point, I should help to finance propaganda directed against my own class.'

'Come now!' exclaimed Don Camillo. 'Have I ever supported propaganda against landowners?'

'Father, I'm not speaking of you personally. I refer simply to what I read in your newspapers and the speeches made by your senators and deputies to parliament.'

'The Church has neither senators nor deputies!' Don Camillo protested.

'That isn't the way you sounded around election time,' said Filotti calmly.

Don Camillo's second stop was at the house of Valerti, who listened quietly to all he had to say and then likewise shook his head.

'Why should I give you money?' he asked. 'It would mean that those of us whom you call "neo-Fascists" would be blasted from two pulpits instead of one.'

Without seeking to defend himself, Don Camillo continued his rounds, but his third visit was no more fortunate than the other two, for Signora Meghini hardly waited for him to end his plea before she started violently shaking her head.

'Father, if you're looking for money with which to open a second church, go to the Republicans. Don't forget that you refused Absolution to all of us who voted for the Monarchist Party.'

Don Camillo went next to Moretti, a landowner of pronounced clerical tendencies. Moretti listened piously to all he had to say, and answered with a sigh:

'Since you speak of the Bishop, I can't say no. But mind you, it's only for his sake.'

'Very good,' said Don Camillo, 'but why must you tell me that only the good Bishop inspires you? Have I failed to please you in some way.'

'Not you personally,' said Moretti, shaking his head. 'But generally speaking, I can't approve of combating Communism by attacking the upper class.'

Don Camillo pocketed Moretti's contribution and went to knock at still another door. Perini opened it in person and gave him ill-humoured attention.

'There's not much I can do, Father,' he said. 'My family just manages to get along, from day to day. Here's my mite, but let's hope that the new priest is up-to-date.'

'Up-to-date?' exclaimed Don Camillo. 'What *do* you mean?'

'It's time people got it into their heads that the world is turning definitely to the Left. We militant Catholics insist upon a social programme, and until the clergy catches up with us, Communism will continue to gain ground. And Communism's no joke, Don Camillo. Don't go imagining that all Communists are like Peppone!'

Don Camillo said that he imagined nothing of the sort, and went to knock at the next door. He made a hundred or more visits, and everywhere he received a reply like one of those quoted above. After several days of going from place to place he unburdened himself to the crucified Christ on the main altar.

'Lord,' he said, 'the rich reproach me for championing the poor, the poor accuse me of conniving with the rich; the whites call me black, the blacks call me white; to the reactionaries I'm a subversive, and to the radicals I'm an obstacle to progress; and as for the Reds, they won't listen to me at all. Am I truly the most ineffective of God's ministers?'

Christ sighed and then answered:

'Don Camillo, you're a skilled hunter and fisherman, aren't you?'

'Yes, Lord.'

'You hunt with a gun and fish with a hook and line, don't you?'

'Yes, Lord.'

'Then if one day you were to see fish flying through the sky and birds slithering under water, would you still fish with a hook and line and hunt with a gun?'

'No, Lord, I'd fish with a gun and hunt with a hook and line.'

'That's where you're wrong, Don Camillo! Because you'd fail completely in both endeavours.'

'Lord, I don't understand.'

'Many do not understand, Don Camillo, because they look at mere words instead of realities.'

Don Camillo collected only enough money to repair the roof of the abandoned church, and it was with a heavy heart that he reported to the Bishopric.

'Never mind, Don Camillo,' said Monsignor Contini. 'Divine Providence will take care of the rest.'

And indeed, after Don Camillo had finished patching the roof, money came from the city for the rest of the repairs. As soon as the work was all done he went to give the good news to Monsignor Contini.

'Then next Sunday you can celebrate the first regular mass at the renovated church,' the Monsignor told him.

Don Camillo's face lit up with joy.

'Monsignore, does that mean you're going to leave me in charge?'

'No, Don Camillo, that would make too heavy a load for you to handle. The new curate is to join you to-morrow. But for a while you'll officiate at the "Bridge" church, while he takes your place in the village. After that, you'll take turns for a while, before settling upon a definitive division of labour.'

'I don't see the reason for so many changes, Monsignore.'

'That's not hard to understand. I know the mentality of your village people. They have a mistrustful and hostile attitude towards anything new. The faithful from the outskirts would be quite capable of making the arduous trip to the centre of the village rather than go to a mass celebrated by a *new* priest. But if you are there for the first few Sundays, they'll surely come. Then, when they've fallen into the habit of going to the renovated church, they'll continue to do so after your assistant has taken it over. The Bishop wants you to follow this procedure.'

'May I speak to His Grace?' asked Don Camillo, humbly bowing his head.

'His Grace is very ill. He must have complete rest.'

'I'd only like to wish him well.'

'He can't talk to anyone. Even listening tires him. The doctor's orders are that he is not to talk or listen or read. Yes, the good man is seriously ill.'

Don Camillo sighed.

'Where is the Bishop's room?' asked Don Camillo. 'As I go out, I'd like to look up at his window.'

'It's on the third floor, but the window gives on to the courtyard, so that no noise can disturb him. I'll try to find a propitious moment for conveying your good wishes to him.'

'Thank you, Monsignore,' said Don Camillo, bowing his head.

'When the new curate arrives, I trust you'll give him a hearty welcome and tell him about the local political situation. He's an extremely capable young man, and up-to-the-minute on social problems.'

'Yes, Monsignore.'

Don Camillo went slowly down the majestic stairs. When he reached the empty front hall he paused for a moment to look into the courtyard, surrounded by arcades, like those of a convent or monastery. The entrance to the courtyard was just across from the front door, and Don Camillo pushed it open and went in. The courtyard garden was untidy, filled with snow, and surrounded by high walls. Don Camillo raised his eyes to look at the long row of windows on the third floor. Which one, he wondered, belonged to the old Bishop? Behind the blackened trunk of a withered tree, he waited for some sign of life from the third floor. But nothing moved, and after lingering for some time, he went away, with his feet soaked from the snow and a chill in his heart.

The New Curate

AT nine o'clock the sky abandoned its ambiguous and threatening air; the clouds were brushed away and the sun's honest face started beaming. After the unseasonably stormy weather which had prevailed all through the spring, Don Camillo at last found cause to rejoice as he hoed his garden. But his joy was short-lived, for the bell-ringer's mother came to disturb him.

'Father, the young curate has come,' she announced.

Don Camillo was prepared for the shock and took it with apparent nonchalance.

'Bring him along, then,' he said, still intent upon his hoeing.

The old woman looked perplexed.

'I just showed him into the hall,' she muttered.

'Well, since I'm not in the hall, but out in the garden, show him out here.'

The old woman went away and a few minutes later the young priest was standing at Don Camillo's side.

'Good day, Father,' he said.

Don Camillo straightened up, and the young priest added:

'I'm Don Gildo.'

'Very happy to see you, I'm sure,' said Don Camillo, giving him a handshake powerful enough to strangle a boa constrictor.

The young priest paled, but he had been instructed in sports and sportsmanship, and so he managed to smile.

'I have a letter from the Bishop's secretary,' he said, holding out a large envelope.

'If you don't mind, I'll look at it right away,' said Don Camillo, taking the letter out of the envelope. After he had finished reading it, he added: 'I told the Bishop's secretary that I was still able to carry on. But since it is the Bishop's will to relieve me of part of my burden, then there's nothing I can do but bid you a hearty welcome.'

Don Gildo bowed politely.

'Thank you, Don Camillo. I am at your service.'

'Those are kind words; I have something for you to do at once.'

He went over to the cherry-tree, took down a hoe that was hanging from one of the branches, and put it into the young priest's hands.

'Two of us can finish the job more than twice as quickly as one,' he observed.

The young priest stared first at the hoe and then at Don Camillo.

'To tell the truth,' he stammered, 'I've no experience of instruments of this kind.'

'That doesn't matter. Stand beside me and do exactly what I do.'

The young priest flushed with annoyance. He was sensitive, and besides, he had his dignity.

'Father,' he said, 'I have come to look after souls, not gardens.'

'Of course,' said Don Camillo calmly. 'But if we are to have fresh fruit and vegetables on our humble table, then the garden must receive some looking after.'

He went on hoeing, while the young man continued to stand helplessly beside him.

'Well,' said Don Camillo at last, 'you mean you really won't help this poor, feeble old man?'

'It's not that I don't want to help you,' the other protested. 'But the fact is that I came here as a priest.'

'The first requisite of the priesthood is humility,' said Don Camillo.

The young priest clenched his teeth and started, somewhat ferociously, to lay about him with the hoe.

'Don Gildo,' observed Don Camillo mildly, 'if I have offended you, take out your resentment on me rather than on this innocent ground.'

The young man made an effort to wield the hoe more gently. It took two hours to finish the work. When the two priests, splattered with mud up to their knees, came back to the rectory, it was eleven o'clock.

'We've just time to do another little job,' said Don Camillo, leading the way to the shed, where there were some elm logs to be sawed.

Not before noon did Don Camillo call a halt. The young man had stored up so much bile in the last three hours that he had no inclination to touch his food. After a single spoonful of soup, he pushed the bowl away.

'Don't worry if you seem to have lost your appetite,' Don Camillo told him. 'It's the change of air.'

Don Camillo had a tremendous appetite himself, and after he had cleaned up two big bowls of vegetable soup with salt pork, he resumed the conversation.

'How do you like the place?' he asked.

'I've hardly had a glimpse of it,' the young man replied.

'It's a village just like any other,' Don Camillo told him, 'with good people and bad. The only difficulty is in telling which is which. As far as politics goes, the Reds are very strong. And the trouble is they seem to be getting stronger. I've tried everything possible, but things continue to worsen.'

'It's all a question of method,' the young man assured him.

'Have you a new method better than the old?' Don Camillo asked curiously.

'I don't mean to make any comparison, and I don't pretend to have found a sure cure. But I do say that we must approach the question from a fresh point of view, or at least without the blinkers which have prevented us from seeing social realities. Why are the Communists so successful among the lower classes? Because they say to them: "Come with us if you want to be better off; we take away from the rich and give to the poor. The priests promise you pie in the sky, but we invite you to cut yourselves a slice here on earth."'

Don Camillo threw out his arms.

'Quite so, Don Gildo, but we can't embrace the materialistic point of view.'

'That isn't necessary. We must cease creating the impression that we defend the status quo. We must speak of rights as well as duties. Of course, if everyone did his duty, he would automatically respect his neighbour's rights. But we have to assert the rights of the poor in order to compel the rich to do their duty. That way, Communism will cease to have any meaning.'

Don Camillo nodded gravely.

'Very true. In other words, we should compete with the Communists on their own ground, even to the point of breaking the law of the land.'

'Exactly. When the law of the land upholds privilege and permits poverty, then it is contrary to justice and hence to divine law.'

Don Camillo threw open his arms.

'My dear Don Gildo, I can follow your train of thought, but I'm too old to adapt myself to it. I haven't the mental agility any longer. You'll have to forgive me.'

Because the curate's mental agility was youthfully intact he poured out a stream of big words, expressive of concepts that were startlingly new. He was aware, moreover, of having a definite mission.

'Father, we know where we're going, and we shall surely attain our goal. You've done a remarkable job, under truly difficult circumstances, and it's high time you had someone to help you. And I don't mean only to help you hoe your garden or saw wood.'

'Forgive me,' said Don Camillo humbly. 'I had no idea how widely read and excellently trained you were.'

The curate had scored a conspicuous triumph. That very afternoon he began making his own contacts in the village and laying plans for future action.

Three days later Don Camillo said to his new assistant:

'You came at just the right moment. I need a complete rest. If it isn't too much for you, I wish you'd take my place entirely for a while. The weather has got me down. I need warmth and dry air, and for months it's done nothing but rain.'

This suited the curate perfectly. He answered enthusiastically that Don Camillo should have no worry at all, for he would shoulder everything, gladly. And so Don Camillo went into retirement. He went no farther than the second floor of the rectory, whose two large rooms looked out, one over the garden and the other over the sports field. The bell-ringer's old mother brought him his food, and he stayed there, in complete seclusion. In one room he had his bed and in the other a small field altar where he said mass every day, all alone, but very close to God. He had brought up a box of books and spent a great part of the time reading. After two weeks had gone by the old woman broke her habitual silence and said:

'Don Camillo, as soon as you feel up to it, come back downstairs. The new curate is making plenty of trouble.'

'Trouble? He seems like a very quiet young man.'

'Quiet? He's not a priest, he's a permanent political rally. Lots of people are staying away from church.'

'Don't let yourself be disturbed. New days, new ways. They'll get used to him in the long run.'

But the new ways really weren't going over, and a few days later the bell-ringer's mother made a new report, which epitomized the whole situation.

'Father, do you know what Peppone said yesterday? He said that as soon as Don Gildo succeeded in emptying the church completely, he'd take him on as group chaplain.'

After another interval of a few days, she informed Don Camillo of the answer Filotti had given to somebody who asked why he hadn't been seen at mass lately. 'I'd rather go and listen to the harangues Peppone gives in the People's Palace. He's not nearly so insulting.'

Don Camillo held his counsel as long as he could. But after forty days he knelt down impatiently in front of the crucifix on the camp altar and said:

'Lord, I bowed humbly to the Bishop's will. I withdrew in order to give Don Gildo complete freedom. You know, Lord, how much I've suffered all this time. Forgive me if I go downstairs, take Don Gildo by the scruff of his neck and dispatch him back to the city.'

It was eight o'clock in the morning, and because Don Camillo wanted to look his best when he finally put in an appearance, he decided to shave. Throwing open the shutters, he discovered that it was a radiantly beautiful day. He paused to take in the peace of the sunlit scene. But a minute later he heard a loud noise. He drew back, but continued to look out at the boys of the 'Invincible' soccer team as they ran nimbly on to the field and started at once on a practice game. Forgetting his beard, he watched them play, but to his sorrow they were far below standard and continually fumbled the ball.

'If they play that way against Peppone's team, they'll take a terrible beating,' he reflected.

Just then Don Gildo ran out on to the field and stopped the game in order to confabulate with the players.

'So he's going to ruin my team as well as everything else,' roared Don Camillo. 'If he doesn't decamp, I'll smash him into small pieces!'

But the curate seemed to have no intention of vacating the centre of the field. At a certain point he took over the captain's place and with the ball between his feet, embarked upon a breathtaking display. Don Camillo cast prudence to the winds and flew, rather than walked, down the stairs. When he reached the field he took Don Gildo by the collar and hauled him into the rectory.

'Take off your cassock, put on a jersey and a pair of heavy shoes, and go on with your coaching!'

'How can I?' the curate stammered.

'Wear long trousers, a mask, and a fake moustache, if you insist, but go ahead and play! You've got to lick that team into shape.'

'But my mission, Father . . .'

'Your mission is to secure a victory of our team over the Reds. That will be a knock-out blow.'

The 'Invincibles' shattered the Red 'Dynamos' and made mincemeat out of them. They celebrated madly, while Peppone and his team were in the dumps. That evening Don Camillo gave a banquet in honour of the curate. After it was over he said:

'From now on, forget about your social programme and concentrate on the soccer team. I'll look after the Communist menace!'

The Champion

RENZO was the sort of fellow that for twenty-five years had jumped on to his racing cycle every morning and ridden all the way to the city to buy the daily *Sport Gazzette*. Of course, he could have bought it on the village square a little later in the day, but that wouldn't have given him the same joy. To pedal fifteen miles to the city and back was his only regular occupation. The rest of the time he was ready to accept any odd job he could get, as long as it allowed him time to buy his paper and read the section concerned with cycling.

Renzo wasn't touched in the head and he wasn't a loafer or a drinker. Cycling was his only interest, and he knew everything there was to know about it. Because he devoured not only the cycling section of the *Sport Gazzette*, but every single piece of printed matter on the subject of bicycles and bicycle races that he could lay his hands on. Renzo was forty years old, and during all the twenty-five years that he had been under the sway of this ruling passion people considered him of no account whatsoever.

Then, all of a sudden, thanks to the Marshall Plan for aid to western intellectuals, the television quiz game was imported from the U.S.A. and Renzo's life took a new turn. When he heard that one of the programmes was to feature a cycling expert, he hurried to glue his eyes on the screen at the Molinetto tavern. And when the master of ceremonies opened the sealed envelope and began to read out the cycling questions, Renzo came up with every one of the answers. The first evening, the tavern habitués took a mild interest in what he was saying; the second week, when he continued to say the right thing, their interest grew. Then, the third week, when the questions got really tough and the expert was shut into a cabin, Renzo's quick thinking caused quite a sensation. The final week, the expert fell down badly on the three decisive questions, but Renzo knew better than he, and the tavern habitués were visibly impressed.

'Why, he could be in the big money!' they exclaimed.

This wasn't the end of the story. Another amateur expert was called on to the programme and walked away with the maximum prize. And the Communist mayor of Reggello, where he came from, organized a big reception, with a brass band and speeches, and hailed him as a man who had brought honour and distinction to his native town.

At this point Peppone called his henchmen together.

'Any political party that manages to enroll Renzo will have a big attraction for the masses. Local elections are just round the corner and we need all the votes he can bring in. Renzo has got to join up, cost what it may!'

They discussed the problem far into the night and the next morning, when Renzo was mounting his bicycle to ride to the city, he found Brusco, Bigio, and Smilzo in his way.

'Renzo,' they said, 'why don't you join the Communist Party? We can get you a road-worker's job and give you a new suit into the bargain.'

'I don't want to be mixed up with political parties,' said Renzo, and pedalled away.

The comrades saw that there was no point in pressing him too hard, and so Renzo was able to go and buy the *Gazzette* as usual. But at the Pioppaccia intersection a group of Christian Democrats was lying in wait.

'Renzo,' they said; 'you're a God-fearing man, and you owe it to yourself to join God's party. If you sign up, we'll get you a job at a garage and a new suit of clothes.'

But Renzo shook his head.

'I joined God's Party when I was baptized,' he retorted.

The stakes were high, and there were hard-headed men on both sides. When the Reds made their second attack they had more to offer: the post of road-work inspector, a suit, an overcoat, and a dozen handkerchiefs.

The Christian Democrats were not slow to match them, holding out not only the job at a garage and the suit of clothes, but an overcoat, a raincoat, a dozen handkerchiefs, and six pairs of stockings as well. This moved Peppone to come forward with a desperate last-minute bid: a brand-new racing cycle. After which, their rivals could propose no less than a motor-scooter.

'Choose any make you like,' they said to Renzo, 'and we'll foot the bill.'

'No,' was Renzo's reply.

At this point they lost patience and their leader said shrilly:

'What the devil *do* you want, then? A car?'

'I don't want anything,' explained Renzo. 'I don't give a hang about political parties. I get round very well on my bicycle, and I don't need either an overcoat or a raincoat.'

By this time the espionage and counter-espionage departments had had ample time to function. The Reds were acquainted with the Christian Democrats' tactics, and vice versa. Since Renzo showed no signs of giving in, and all the while television quizzes were becoming more and more popular, Peppone disregarded his position in the Party and fell back on that of mayor. He called representatives of all the democratic parties to a meeting in the town-hall and addressed them as follows:

'My fellow-citizens! When the spiritual and material assets of the community are at stake, partisan politics must take a back seat. We have gathered together out of concern for the general welfare, and I am speaking as one of you. The achievements of the champion from Reggello and the praise given him by his mayor point to the necessity of forming a non-partisan committee to present our candidate for television honours and win for ourselves the same glory.'

These stirring words met with loud applause, and the committee turned out to have five Communist and five Christian Democrat members. They went to work at once and closed their first session with a highly satisfactory order of the day. The next morning they went in a body to Renzo's house and set forth the situation.

'Renzo, this is no question of politics or political parties. It involves the interests of the whole village, not to mention your own. You must get on the next television quiz. We'll start the ball rolling, somehow or other, and put you over. Because the good name of the village is at stake, we'll get you a whole outfit of new clothes, send you to Milan by car and give you some cash besides. That way you can win the prize money and our village will be in the headlines. Besides, the *Sport Gazzette* is published in Milan and you'll be able to get it hot off the press.'

But Renzo only shook his head.

'The *Gazzette* I buy in the nearest city is quite good enough for me. I don't have to go all the way to Milan.'

'And what about the money? You're not too high-and-mighty for that, are you?'

'I said I didn't want to get mixed up in politics, didn't I?' said Renzo.

'But this isn't a matter of politics. No one's asking you to join any party.'

Renzo continued to shake his head.

'Five of you offered me a road-work job, and the other five a job in a garage. I simply don't trust you.'

The next step was logical enough. Peppone with his five Reds and Piletti with his five Blacks converged upon the rectory. Don Camillo greeted them with considerable perplexity.

'Father,' said Peppone, 'I am speaking as first citizen of the village and representative of all the rest. You're the only man who can convince Renzo that it's not politics, but a matter concerning the village reputation. He has a good chance of winning the jackpot of the television quiz programme and so he simply *must* compete for it.'

Don Camillo stared at him with amazement.

'Do you mean to say that you want to put the village idiot on the air?'

'Who else is there?' said Peppone. 'You, Father? Do you know when and in what race Girardengo had cramps in his right leg?'

'No, I don't,' admitted Don Camillo.

'Well, we need a fellow that knows just this kind of thing. And that means Renzo. He may very well win the big prize.'

'What? Renzo win five million liras?'

At this point Piletti, the leader of the Christian Democrats, intervened:

'Father,' he said with some annoyance, 'I'm afraid I'll have to remind you of something you surely know, since it isn't among the rules of the quiz contest: "Blessed are the poor in spirit, for theirs is the kingdom of heaven." '

'Come, come,' Don Camillo retorted; 'I have a distinction to make there. The Gospel doesn't tell us that the "poor in spirit" are village idiots.'

'This is no time to bicker about trifles,' put in Peppone. 'You know perfectly well how things stand, and it's your job to tell Renzo that politics don't enter into them.'

Don Camillo threw out his arms and exclaimed:

'May the people's will be done!'

'Renzo,' the priest said. 'If I guarantee that politics has no part in this affair of the television quiz, will you believe me?'

'Yes, Father.'

'And if I give you my word of honour that they want to help you only in order that you may win the big money and put our village in the public eye, will you believe me?'

'Yes, Father.'

'Then accept their offer, and sign up for the quiz.'

'No, Father.'

Don Camillo was frankly puzzled.

'Renzo, you simply don't want to be quizzed. Tell me why.'

'Because I have my dignity, Father.'

Don Camillo did not insist. He paced up and down the room and then came to stand with outspread legs right in front of his interlocutor.

'Renzo, if you're giving up all that money, you deserve some recompense. I'll hire you as bell-ringer.'

Renzo was taken with this idea. What more suitable occupation could he hope to find? He thought it over for five whole minutes and then shook his head.

'I can't do it, Father. The bells have to be rung in the morning, and that's when I go to the city to buy the *Sport Gazzette*.'

'But exactly the same paper is sold here!' shouted Don Camillo.

Renzo laughed.

'No, Father; the city paper is an entirely different thing. . . .'

In matters of stubbornness Don Camillo was something of an expert but in this case all he could do was mutter some semi-biblical phrases about the stiff-necked race of sport fans.

The Carburettor

THE newspapers were still full of the story of the child whose life had been saved by the miracle drugs sent by plane from America. Even after the child had recovered they continued to feature the story. According to the Hammer-and-Sickle crowd, it was nothing but a propaganda stunt cooked up by the United States ambassadress.

It all happened in a village on the big river, some twenty miles from the parish of Don Camillo, and so when the dispute was at its hottest Peppone felt he must step in, in order, as he said, 'to protect the good reputation of the lower Po valley'. His version of the tale was embroidered with so much fancy that Don Camillo found it necessary to run into him – by sheer chance, of course – under the arcade in front of the café, just as he was holding forth on the whys and wherefores of the miraculous cure. As soon as Peppone saw the priest's bulky form looming on the horizon he raised his voice to announce:

'Of course, where political propaganda is concerned, anything goes. But there is a limit to everything, and when it comes to exploiting a helpless child, I draw the line. Any family man will understand what I mean, but naturally one that wears a long black skirt and has no hope of having any children can't be expected to realize. . . .'

The bystanders turned to look at Don Camillo, and feeling their eyes upon him, he nonchalantly shrugged his shoulders.

'Mr Mayor,' he said blandly, 'if the patient was a child, there was no way of saving an adult, was there?'

'What do you mean by "save"?' retorted Peppone. 'There was never any real danger.'

'Well, if you're a medical authority, I've nothing more to say.'

'I never claimed to be a medical authority,' said Peppone. 'But specialists stated that there was no need to bring the medicine from overseas when it was available in Holland.'

'I'm quite willing to bow to the specialists' opinion. But there's one detail which you and the rest of the comrades seem to have overlooked. The baby didn't need the milk of a contented Dutch cow or the air flailed by a Dutch windmill. He had to have a certain gamma globule which is the exclusive property of the state of Michigan, so why shouldn't the United States ambassadress send there for it?'

Peppone shook his head and laughed loudly.

'*Latinorum latinorum!* When they're at their wit's end they come out with their *latinorum*, their *alpha* and *gamma* and *omega* and all the rest, and if you're not a Latin scholar, you can't reply.'

'Mr Mayor, *gamma* is a Greek letter and not a Latin one. And anyhow, scientists rather than priests gave this haemoglobin its name.'

'Very well,' said Peppone, pulling another Soviet propaganda card out of his sleeve, 'but what about the Madonna that appeared to the child in a dream? Didn't the priests think up that one?'

'Mr Mayor,' said Don Camillo, with an expression of astonishment on his face, 'the clergy does not interfere with children's dreams, or with those of adults, either. They dream when and what they please.'

'Listen to this, though,' shouted Peppone. 'While the plane commandeered by that platinum fox of an ambassadress was flying over the Atlantic, the sick child did dream. And what did he dream about? The Madonna! In his dream the Madonna carried him to Paradise and introduced Jesus Christ, who said that thanks to the United States and Clare Booth Luce, the story would be crowned by a happy ending.'

'What was the child to dream, Mr Mayor?' asked Don Camillo, throwing out his arms in resignation. 'Was Lenin to carry him off to the Kremlin and Stalin to explain the Five-year Plan?'

Someone in the group laughed and Peppone grew angrier than ever.

'Let's keep politics out of it!' he exclaimed. 'We'd never saddle a child with a dream of this kind. First, because we don't make propaganda out of children, and second, because we don't have to resort to fairy stories. . . .'

'. . . And third, because no one would believe them if you did,' Don Camillo concluded.

'And who believes *your* fairy stories, may I ask?'

'There are people, quite a few of them, who not only believe in Paradise, but are willing to behave in such a way as to go there, people that live good, quiet lives and trust in Divine Providence.'

Peppone pushed his hat back on his head and placed his hands on his hips.

'Divine Providence, eh? When the medicine came from the U.S.A.! If it had come from Russia, the Reverend here would have said it was a work of the devil!'

'No, Mr Mayor. The Reverend, as you call him, uses

his God-given faculty of reason. He'd never say anything quite so stupid, because he knows that Divine Providence knows neither nation nor party.'

'Amen,' muttered Smilzo.

'In any case,' Don Camillo continued, 'this time Divine Providence came from the West rather than the East.'

'Then hurrah for America, and down with Russia!' shouted Peppone.

'Hurrah for America, if you insist. But why down with Russia? Russia did no harm in this affair; Russia didn't prevent the child from getting well. I am quite capable of cool detachment, Mr Mayor, and I'm not afraid to say that this is one instance – perhaps the only one – in which Russia did no damage whatsoever. But, Mr Mayor, instead of yelling Hurrah for America, why not yell Hurrah for Divine Providence, since Divine Providence cured the child?'

Peppone was as red in the face as the October Revolution.

'Why didn't Divine Providence stop the child from getting sick, in the first place?' he asked.

'Divine Providence didn't bring about the sickness,' Don Camillo explained. 'Sickness is a product of Nature, and Nature is governed, fortunately, by very rigid laws. If we fail to observe them, then trouble is bound to ensue. As a skilled mechanic, you know, Mr Mayor, that a motor runs smoothly just as long as its single parts are in good order. If a carburettor is out of order, is it the fault of Divine Providence or of the dirt that got into it? Everything connected with Matter is in the providence of Nature. There is sickness even in Russia, which was created not by God but by Lenin.'

Peppone had gradually relaxed and at the end of Don Camillo's little harangue he turned to Smilzo and said with a smile, pronouncing every word slowly:

'Smilzo, apropos of the carburettor, would you ask

the Reverend whether when this mechanic gets the dirt out of the carburettor he represents Divine Providence?'

Smilzo looked over at Don Camillo, and asked:

'Has the defendant heard the plaintiff's demand?'

'Yes,' Don Camillo replied. 'The plaintiff's complaint is a weakness of the brain, but at any rate the defendant has heard it. The mechanic doesn't represent Divine Providence; all he represents is a screwdriver, with a man attached to the handle. All this lies in the realm of the very lowliest kind of matter. Everything happens in accord with natural rather than divine law.'

This reply seemed to give Peppone further satisfaction.

'Let's put it differently, Father,' he said. 'Let's say that the carburettor isn't working for lack of a screw. Unfortunately, it's an American carburettor, and we haven't the right screw to replace it. What are we to do? Scrap the car? Fortunately the United States ambassadress sends a plane to Washington to get it; the screw is put in and the car moves. We're still in the realm of matter, because a humble carburettor is the protagonist of our story. But since the new screw comes from the U.S.A. we must shout Hurrah for Divine Providence. If the carburettor comes from the East you reason one way, and if it comes from the West another.'

Peppone's gang hooted their approval, and Don Camillo let them hoot to their hearts' content. Then he said:

'My reason works the same way in both directions.'

'Bunk!' shouted Peppone. 'If the child's sickness is the result of natural law, just as the carburettor is broken for lack of a screw, then why is Divine Providence responsible for the American ambassadress's offer of the missing part, or, in this case, the missing medicine?'

'Because a child isn't a carburettor, that's all,' said Don Camillo calmly. 'A carburettor can't have a child's faith in God. And this child gave proof of his faith in a spectacular way. The human machine, its disturbances and remedies are material and natural affairs. Faith in God is something quite different, which you, Comrade Carburettor, seem unable to understand. Instead of seeing Divine Providence, you see only the United States ambassadress and the Atlantic Pact. A man without hearing can't hope to understand music, and one without faith in God can't fathom the workings of Divine Providence.'

'Well then, this Divine Providence is something for the privileged rather than the needy. If a hundred persons are starving and only seven of them have faith, then God is unjust to send a tin of Spam only to these seven.'

'No, Comrade Mayor, God sends the Spam to the whole lot of them, but only seven possess a tin-opener, with which the rest will have nothing to do.'

Peppone had once more lost his self-possession and was sweating under the collar.

'Father, let's drop the parable and look at reality. In our country only seven people out of a hundred and seven eat meat, because they believe in Divine Providence and have the tin-openers with which to get at it. Whereas in Russia, where nobody believes in Divine Providence, there are tin-openers for all.'

'But no tins of Spam,' said Don Camillo.

The bystanders laughed at Don Camillo's thrust and Peppone was beside himself with fury.

'You're clever at playing with words, Father, and you reduce every argument to a word game. But we have concrete facts for our premises. This whole thing is a political trick, an American propaganda stunt built round an innocent child. None of your big words have proved the contrary.'

'I know,' said Don Camillo, with a shrug of his shoulders. 'I'll never be able to prove a thing to you, not even that two and two make four, because you've been taught that they make five. I can tell you this, though.

If political propaganda saved a child's life, then I say Hurrah for political propaganda. If I had a child and his life depended on some Russian medicine, I can assure you that I . . .'

'Not I,' Peppone interrupted. 'I have children, but if their lives depended on medicine flown in by the United States ambassadress, I'd let them die!'

Don Camillo only opened his eyes wide in horror.

At three o'clock in the morning Peppone was still unable to sleep. He got up and dressed, then with his shoes in his hand went to peer into his young son's room. He switched on the light and scrutinized the child's face. After some time he put out the light and tiptoed away. A few minutes later, with his coat collar raised all the way to his eyes, he walked through the icy streets to the church square. Under the rectory windows he stooped to look for a stone, but the hardened snow had stuck them all to the ground. He scratched at the frozen ground and with every passing minute his anxiety grew. Finally he loosened a stone and threw it at the shutters of the second window from the left of the second floor. The sound that it made when it struck the shutters was somehow reassuring. The shutters were thrown open and a rough voice called down:

'What do you want?'

'Come downstairs.'

Don Camillo draped the bedspread over his shoulders and came to open the door.

'What can you want at this hour? What's the matter?'

'Nothing's the matter,' said Peppone glumly.

'Good. When I first saw you I was afraid.'

'Afraid of what? I'm not a burglar.'

'I'm always afraid when someone rouses me at night. People don't come to see a priest at an hour like this just in order to tell him a funny story.'

Peppone stood with lowered head for a minute and then mumbled:

'When a fellow holds a public discussion, he often says more than he means.'

'I know,' said Don Camillo. 'There's no use taking such things too seriously.'

'But other people take them seriously.'

'Nonsense! They know what kind of reasoning to expect from a carburettor.'

Peppone clenched his fists.

'Father, you're the one that's talking stupidly.'

'You may be right. But then a carburettor has no right to wake up a priest at three o'clock in the morning.'

Peppone stood his ground until the priest asked him:

'Is there something you want, Comrade Peppone? Do you need a tin-opener?'

'I have a tin-opener,' said Peppone gloomily.

'Good! See that you don't lose it. And may God shed a little more light upon you next time you talk in public!'

Peppone went away, and before Don Camillo got back into bed he knelt down before the crucifix in his room.

'Lord,' he said, 'he hasn't become a carburettor, or anything else soulless and purely mechanical. He's just the same poor fellow that he was before. May Divine Providence be praised!'

And then he, too, was at last able to go to sleep.

The Closed Gate

THE highway unrolls its asphalt ribbon along the bank,
matching the peaceful flow of the river. But the tributary
roads which run into it, although they come from an
area as flat as a billiard-table, are tortuous and winding. A city driver, bitten by the mania for speed, would
find them unutterably irritating, but they exactly suit
a man who works his own land and is jealous of its
boundaries.

The Quarta road, doubtless a former cow-path, is
such a one. Just a few hundred yards beyond the village
it leaves the northbound highway and winds its way for
five miles or so before rejoining it, only one mile farther
on. The last section of it runs parallel to both highway
and river, then, just half a mile away from the junction,
it makes a right-angle turn and climbs straight up the
bank. The farm known as the *Cantone* is there at the turn,
with the road bounding it on two sides and the farm
buildings right at the corner.

The curve is a dangerously blind one, and because the
Quarta road runs by a number of properties and is the

only line of communication between the village and the outlying community of Torricella, it is heavily travelled. The farmhouse is at the side of the road just before the right-angle turn to the east, and the barns, which are joined to it, just after. Between them lies the bare, rectangular barnyard, open towards the south and towards the river. The main entrance to the farm was originally at the south-east corner of the house.

All these topographical details serve only to explain something very simple: if some luckless fellow were to come carelessly out of the barnyard and another, equally luckless, were to drive at top speed towards the curve, it was obvious that they might run straight into each other. Something of the sort did happen, and as a result the gate was closed and creeper allowed to grow over it.

Marco Stocci had inherited the farm from his father, after many years of working at his side. Now he continued to work, with his wife and one hired man to help him. He was forty years old, but he had married late and Gisa, the eldest of his three children, was only just over twelve years old. With this family to bring up and a large amount of land to till, it is not surprising that Marco was a difficult and sometimes intractable man. He had an exceedingly quick temper and if his children annoyed him, he struck out at them with a violence which might have caused pain even to a grown person. The two little boys, eight and ten years old, took all this in a sporting spirit and were careful only to stay out of his reach. But twelve-year-old Gisa had a more sentimental nature and was mortally afraid of her father. Being a delicate and sensitive child she suffered most when he struck her in the presence of strangers, and in this he seemed to take particular joy. The last time that Marco mistreated his daughter was when the barnyard was full of men who had come for the threshing.

The threshing was a meagre affair that year; after an unusually severe winter, the wheat yielded very little grain. Marco Stocci was boiling over with resentment. Every now and then he plunged his hand into the sack hanging under the threshing-machine, pulled out a fistful of grain and then put it back, cursing. There was another major worry on his mind: his best cow was mortally ill and the vet showed no signs of coming. His two sons, aware of the oppressive atmosphere, had taken to the bush, but Gisa had been given the job of carrying water to the men on the machine and could not get away. The vet arrived around noon, when the men had just come in from the fields and were sitting down to lunch, amid considerable confusion. He went to look at the ailing cow, wrote out a prescription, and said to Stocci:

'The pharmacy's closed at this hour. At three o'clock, when it reopens, send someone there to pick up this medicine. I'll be back at four to give the injection.'

While the men lingered over their lunch in the cool hall, Stocci went into the parlour. He remembered that the pharmacist had sent him a bill the month before and it seemed like a good time to pay it. The bill was in a yellow envelope; it came to 4,500 liras, which meant that 10,000 liras would easily cover the present prescription as well as those that had gone before. He put the prescription into a pink envelope, lying on his desk, together with a 10,000-lira note. Then he thought it would be simpler to have everything together, and put it all in the pharmacist's yellow envelope.

It was a hot day, and the men were anxious to finish the threshing early and go on to another job. Stocci had barely enough time to eat a few mouthfuls of lunch and gulp down half a bottle of wine before they were ready to return to work. At half past two, when the machine was just about to swallow up the last bale of wheat, Stocci remembered the vet and the sick cow and called to his daughter:

'Take the yellow envelope from the parlour table and run to the pharmacy. Hand him the envelope and then wait for what he gives you. Hurry!'

Gisa took the envelope and started off, walking alongside her bicycle, as her parents had always told her she should do until she was on the open road. She went through the gate and continued to walk until she was round the dangerous curve. Then she mounted the bicycle and rode to the village by the shortest road, which was that along the bank of the river. When she came back the threshing was over, and while some of the men were making the machine ready to go, the others were cooling off with glasses of wine. Stocci was in the loft, over the sealed door between the house and the barn, and when he saw Gisa arrive with a small parcel attached to the handlebars of her bicycle, he called down from the window:

'Have you got everything?'

'Yes, father.'

'How much change did he give you?'

'What change?' she stammered.

'Change from the 10,000 liras that were in the envelope!'

'There were two sheets of paper in the envelope, and nothing more,' she said, shaking her head.

Money is a sore subject where a peasant is concerned, because it is so very hard for him to come by. It's safer to cut off his ear than to touch his money. And so Stocci let out a loud cry.

'Nothing more! I put the money in with my own hand! And now you've gone and lost it, you little good-for-nothing! If you don't find it, I'll kill you!'

Blind anger made the veins stand out on his forehead and muddled his brain. Not content with shouting, he started to climb down the wooden ladder up which he was later to carry sacks of wheat. And Gisa, instead of waiting for him, fled in terror. She jumped on to the bicycle and pedalled furiously in the direction of the gate. Her father ran after her, but she had a head start, and had already reached the road. The road was covered with gravel, and as she turned to the right, she lost control and went off to the extreme left, at the edge of the ditch. Just then a truck roared down the road at full speed, and as it cleared the curve Gisa was directly in its way. She was killed on the spot, in plain sight of her father.

This was why Stocci closed the gate to his farm. He fastened it with a heavy chain and lock, and put the key in his pocket so that no one could ever go through the gate again. The portion of the highway which ran parallel to the country road, some hundred and fifty feet away, was connected with it at another place, where there was no blind corner. The creeper, which formerly had covered only the gate-posts, now ran over all the iron grating. After a month had gone by, Stocci re-covered a measure of calm. He was not very different from what he had been before, but he no longer shouted, and he let his wife look after the little boys.

One of the gate-posts was up against the corner of the house, while the other marked the beginning of the hedge which separated the barnyard from the road. Beside the latter post grew a tall poplar tree, and in the summer Stocci sat in its shade looking out through the over-grown bars of the closed gate at the dusty, white road, with the sun beating upon it.

It was an August afternoon, and the air was particularly heavy. Almost everyone was asleep in the river valley, and silence and solitude reigned. Stocci sat under the tree, staring at the gate. Suddenly someone rode up the road on a bicycle and stopped directly in front of it. The leaves had grown so thick that Stocci could not make out who it was. He got up and went nearer. It was Gisa, staring at him out of her deep blue eyes. Stocci searched his vest pocket for the key. The lock was so rusty that the key was hard to turn, and it was no easy job to tear away the vine, but there was a feverish strength in Stocci's hands and soon he had the gate open.

'Come in,' he said to his daughter, but she only shook her head, remounted the bicycle, and rode off towards the fatal curve.

For a minute Stocci could not move. But when she was out of sight he ran back to his own bicycle, which was leaning against the wall of the house. He leaped on to the saddle and pedalled out through the open gate, just as fast as Gisa had pedalled to her death before him. He skidded on the gravel and veered to the left just in time for the luckless driver coming round the curve to find him in his way and run him down.

It was two o'clock in the afternoon, and old Antonietta, whose insomnia made her the only person left awake in the heat, swore that she saw Stocci and Gisa riding their bicycles along the road in front of her house. They rode side by side, in true cyclists' fashion, and every now and then they looked at each other and smiled.

Sheer imagination, of course. But in the secret compartment of Stocci's wallet they found a pink envelope containing the 10,000-lira note which Gisa had never lost because her father, in the confusion, had never put it in with the bill and the prescription. This part of the story is absolutely true, and Stocci's widow gave the 10,000-lira note to Don Camillo.

'Say some masses,' she told him.

'For whose soul?' he asked her.

'For both of them, Father.'

So spake Stocci's widow, and she closed the gate again, this time with the aid of a blow-lamp. After which the creeper resumed its temporarily interrupted process of growing.

Lullaby

PEPPONE sat in front of the fireplace, while his wife and children set the supper-table, at the same time watching the pot and frying-pan on the stove. Just then Smilzo burst into the house with a large rolled-up paper in one hand.

'Here's the corrected proof, Chief,' he said. 'If it's O.K., we're ready to print it.'

'Stand away,' ordered Peppone. 'I want to get the general effect.'

Smilzo stepped several steps back, unrolling the paper. At this distance the poster was most effective. It stated very clearly that a Very Important Party Person would come to the village at three o'clock Saturday afternoon and explain to the citizenry 'the true story of the Hungarian counter-revolution'.

'All right,' said Peppone. 'The posters have got to be up by tomorrow morning.'

After Smilzo had gone away, Peppone's wife said:

'Haven't you killed those poor devils enough by now?'

'What nonsense are you saying?' asked Peppone, wheeling brusquely around.

'It's no nonsense. If you were an honest man, you'd get out in a hurry.'

Peppone was in no mood for an argument and so he turned back to the fire, with one parting shot over his shoulder.

'I'm an honest man. But a soldier can't abandon his post just because the general has changed his tactics. Ours is a just struggle, because we're fighting for the good of the working-class.'

'You don't do much good to the working-class by killing it off,' said his wife severely. 'They weren't capitalists, they were peasants and workers, and students, peasants' and workers' sons.'

'That's all propaganda,' jeered Peppone; 'just the usual line.'

'Propaganda isn't what goes over with me,' said his wife. 'I listen to my conscience, and I'm getting out of the Women's League, I can tell you.'

Peppone wasn't prepared for such a drastic decision, and for a few minutes he was left speechless.

'Keep your mind on the supper,' he said in a surly voice. 'I don't feel like joking.'

'It's no joke,' she retorted, and taking a card out of the top bureau drawer she tore it into tiny pieces and threw them on the table. 'There is my membership,' she said, 'and tomorrow morning I'll go and tell Gisella to take my name off the list.'

Peppone jumped to his feet in a towering rage and shook a fist in his wife's face.

'You'll do no such thing,' he shouted. 'You'll stay right here. I wear the trousers in this house.'

Peppone's wife wasn't a woman to be easily buffaloed. Taking advantage of the fact that she was on the other side of the table from Peppone, she seized the pot and frying-pan off the stove and threw their contents down the sink.

'If you wear the trousers, then eat the supper.'

Such a bit of rebellion would have indisposed the most peaceful of men, and Peppone was anything but peaceful. Because of his bulk and masculine dignity he couldn't very well jump over the table, but he did move with astonishing swiftness to lay hands on his wife. He had counted without her bodyguards, however, and his impetus was checked by four little children crawling around his legs and shattering his eardrums with their cries. A second later his wife had disappeared up the stairs and his pursuit was blocked by the attic door.

'Open up, or I'll break through!' he roared, hammering at it with his fists.

When he received no answer, he threw the full weight of his shoulder against the door and erupted into the attic, which, to his discomfiture, was empty. His wife had climbed through the skylight on to the roof, and there, in spite of the darkness, Peppone finally detected her, hanging on to a chimney. His rage was transformed into worry and he drew back, with cold sweat breaking out on his forehead. Meanwhile the children too had reached the attic, weeping and calling for their mother.

'Shut up and get out of here!' said Peppone irritatedly.

Fearfully they retreated towards the door, until the oldest suddenly broke away from the rest, scuttled up the ladder standing under the skylight, and joined his mother on the roof. With this Peppone turned tail and fled.

When Peppone came home, after midnight, he found things just as he had left them: the table still set and the scraps of the membership card scattered all over it. The big double bed in the bedroom was empty and so were the beds of the children. The rebels, all five of them, had taken refuge in the room which had formerly belonged to his wife's parents. Peppone made a feeble attempt to force the door but soon realized that it was barricaded. Back in the empty, disorderly kitchen, where the fire in the stove was dead and cold, he attempted to stay his appetite with bread and cheese, but they only made his stomach turn over. Before going out again he knocked once more at the rebels' door.

'Tomorrow noon, if I don't find lunch, I'll smash everything in sight.'

'Smash what you please,' his wife answered calmly. 'Either you let me go and see Gisella, or else tomorrow you'll find the house empty.'

Peppone started to kick at the door, but the children's weeping and wailing caused him to desist.

'I said noon, mind you!' he shouted. 'That's the deadline for putting everything in order. I'll go and see Gisella myself. If you resign, we'll have to publish an announcement to the effect that you've been kicked out for deviationism. I've got to settle things in such a way that I won't be a laughing-stock.'

'Go ahead,' said his wife, 'but just don't try to put over anything on me like what they pulled in Budapest!'

Peppone roared for an answer.

Gisella, the fiery head of the Women's League, had, with Don Camillo's accidental assistance, been tinged in red of the deepest hue by the most ferocious of her former adversaries, now her husband. She had turned into a professional politician, which meant that her husband, after working hours, had to do the housekeeping, to cook his meals if he wanted to eat, to make his bed if he wanted to sleep, and to sweep up if he didn't want the place to be a pigsty. Ever since Gisella had become a big wheel of the Party, the poor fellow had lost all his revolutionary spirit. He confined himself to being a good proletarian husband and let politics strictly alone. Indeed, to talk politics in his presence was like referring to rope in the house of a man who has died on the gallows.

At ten o'clock in the morning Peppone went to the People's Palace to hold a private meeting with Gisella upon the subject of his wife's rebellion. But Gisella was at home, ill. In view of the fact that the big rally was to take place at three that afternoon and Gisella was in charge of the women's participation, she must have been very ill indeed or else nothing in the world would have kept her away from the job. And so Peppone went to the forsaken shack where she and her husband lived and found her in bed, looking anything but well.

'What's the matter, Comrade?' he asked her.

Gisella only shook her head sadly, for she had not strength enough to speak.

'Arthritis,' said her husband, who had stayed at home to look after her. 'The poor girl's bones are broken.'

To tell the truth, if Gisella had a bad case of broken bones, arthritis wasn't the reason. It had all happened the previous evening, after supper, a sketchy sort of supper prepared by Gisella's husband while she worked for the second consecutive day on the speech she was scheduled to deliver at the rally. When the comrade from the city had finished telling the true story of the Hungarian counter-revolution, Gisella was to voice the village women's acclaim of the peaceful settlement effected by the glorious Soviet army. Naturally, so important a speech couldn't be improvised from one moment to the next, and by the time Gisella had said everything she had to say, her crude handwriting covered some twenty long pages. At the end of the meagre meal, Gisella's husband sat down by the fire while she put the finishing touches. When it was all done she had an urge to rehearse it.

'Even if you don't care a fig for politics,' she said to her husband, 'you can tell me whether or not my speech makes sense. Just listen . . .'

The poor fellow threw out his arms helplessly, and Gisella launched into her oration. When she got to the end she asked him:

'Well, what do you say?'

He tapped his pipe on one of the bricks of the fireplace, then put it back in his mouth and jerking his chair round said brusquely:

'Eat it.'

'What do you mean?' she asked in amazement.

'I said to eat it,' he repeated, pointing to the pad on which the speech was written. Gisella stood with arms akimbo and looked at him with disgust, as if she were about to put him in his place. But before she could open her mouth she received a stunning blow across the face. The blow was painful, but Gisella was even more pained by the fact that the browbeaten little man should have found the nerve to administer it. The worm had turned at last.

'Eat it,' he said again, following up the first blow with a second.

Gisella didn't understand for some time, but at last it got into her head that if she wanted the blows to let up she would have to eat all twenty pages of her speech and her card of membership in the Women's League as well. That evening Gisella couldn't get up the stairs by herself. Alone, she had received enough blows to fell the entire women's group of the local party. Her rebellious spouse carried her upstairs, as if she had been a sack of potatoes. And that is just about what she was.

Now Peppone told Gisella not to worry. 'While you're recuperating I'll put a substitute in your place. We'll wait for you to get well.'

'She's not going to get well,' said her husband darkly. 'It's a chronic disturbance, isn't it, Gisella?'

Gisella nodded assent.

'It's not really a substitute that I'm putting in,' said Peppone. 'No one can take your place. The best thing is to disband the group and build it up again on a new foundation.'

'I agree,' said the husband.

'Take good care of yourself, Comrade,' said Peppone, moving towards the door. 'The Party needs you.'

'I'll take care of her, don't worry,' said the husband. 'I need her too.'

When Peppone came home at noon, he found everything in good order. He sat down cheerfully at the table, with a whale of an appetite, as his wife knew very well. But she stood skittishly near the sink, holding the bowl of spaghetti in her hand and ready to repeat the gesture of the day before.

'Well?' she queried at last.

'Everything's all right. Gisella is ill and I've had to disband the group.'

He exhibited a copy of the announcement, and in return was served his portion of hot food.

The rally was scheduled for three o'clock in the afternoon, and by two the square and the road leading to the highway were patrolled by a detachment of police sent from the city. It wasn't clear what had drawn out so large and aggressive a crowd. The windows of all the houses were shut and the storekeepers had closed their stores, making the village seem quite dead. At a quarter to three Smilzo arrived breathlessly at the house of Peppone.

'Everything's ready, Chief. The comrades have gathered in the auditorium, and outside all is quiet. The enemy doesn't dare let himself be seen.'

At that very moment, however, the enemy let himself be heard, for from the church tower the death-knell sounded. Deeply and gloomily it tolled against a background of perfect silence. Peppone listened for a few minutes and then said:

'Go back to your place. I'm going to do something about this.'

'Be careful, Chief,' said Smilzo; 'it's a critical moment.'

'In moments like this we must show that we are not afraid.'

He put on his coat, pulled his hat down over his eyes, and hurried off towards the church.

Up in the bell-tower, Don Camillo was pulling intently at the rope when Peppone's head appeared at the trap-door, followed by his body.

'Father,' he said, 'there's got to be an end to this provocation.'

'There's an end to everything,' said Don Camillo. 'In human affairs, nothing is eternal.'

'I can't answer for what may happen.'

'Never mind, Comrade Mayor; I'll answer for it.'

Peppone looked cautiously out of the window. From this height he had a clear view of the empty square, the police car, and the forces of law and order. It was a grey day, and even without the tolling bell there would have been something infinitely lugubrious and funereal about it. Punctually at three o'clock, the Party speaker's car, with its police escort, drew up in front of the cinema.

'Comrade, aren't you going to the rally?' asked Don Camillo, between one sound of the bell and another.

'I want to see for myself exactly how long you'll go on with this music,' said Peppone, sitting down on the floor.

'For a very long time,' said Don Camillo. 'This is no ordinary death; it's the death of a whole people.'

Peppone sat hunched up in one corner with his hat over his eyes. He was dead tired and soon this gloomy lullaby sent him off to sleep. So it was that he never heard the true story of the Hungarian counter-revolution.

Togo the Bull

IT was one of those things that usually come out in the tabloid papers. If it didn't, the reason was that certain ramifications of the affair induced the village people to pretend to have seen and heard nothing.

It was the afternoon of 31 December, and everywhere people were preparing to celebrate the arrival of the New Year. Those who weren't at home were out going from shop to shop or else just loitering in the square. Children had been dashing madly about all day long, whiling away the hours before the climactic noise-making, with the explosion of an occasional firework.

In the Rotti farmyard there was a big band of boys, letting off crackers in this way, in spite of their elders' admonitions. But when it was time to lead the animals out of the stable to water, old man Rotti came into the yard and said that if he heard as much as a squeak, he'd give the whole lot of them a beating. The boys quieted down, and the animals enjoyed their drink. But just when Togo reached the trough, an unfortunate cracker rose up from behind the fence, whistled across the yard, and landed on his nose.

Togo was a Carnation-type bull, a Sherman tank of such massive proportions that the very sight of him was intimidating. With a single leap he broke away from the cowherd, smashed the bars of the gate, and rushed out on to the road. The Rotti farm was hardly outside the village; fifty yards away the road became a village street, leading in a few hundred feet to the square. And by the time the Rottis had recovered from their surprise and started to pursue him, this was where Togo had arrived, or rather erupted. It was a confused scene, and one of only a few minutes' duration. Togo started to vent his wrath on a group of hysterical women, who squeezed themselves into the narrow space between a wall and two big trucks, while the sergeant of the Carabinieri appeared from nowhere and stood in the way with a pistol in his hand.

The sergeant's shot grazed the bull's side and only intensified his anger. It looked as if both the sergeant and the little group of shrieking women were in danger of being trampled down. Only a volley of machine-gun bullets into Togo's brain could have stopped him in his mad course. And, just in the nick of time, there was just such a volley. No one knew where it came from, but it hit the target, and the bull collapsed at the sergeant's feet. He put his pistol back in the holster, took off his cap, and wiped the cold sweat from his forehead, looking down all the while at the great carcass of the bull.

People all around him were making a racket, and the women were shrieking just as loudly as if the bull were still charging upon them, but in the sergeant's ears there rang only the rattle of the machine-gun. The gun was silent now, but he felt sure that he had only to turn round and look up in order to pick out the window from which it had been fired. This was the real reason for his sweating. He knew that he ought to turn and look, but he didn't have the courage to do so.

The sergeant's paralysis was broken by a heavy hand on his shoulder.

'Good for you, Sergeant!' said Don Camillo. 'These people owe you their lives.'

'He's a very brave fellow,' wheezed an old crone who was standing near by, 'but if it hadn't been for . . .'

She meant to say 'for the fellow who fired the machine-gun', but she never finished the sentence because someone stepped on her foot so hard that she almost fainted away, and a moment later the gathering crowd absorbed her.

'Good for you, Sergeant!' everyone was shouting.

Don Camillo went back to the rectory and waited for the sergeant to turn up. After an hour he did free himself and turn up, as expected.

'Father,' he said, 'you're the only person to whom I can say what's on my mind. Will you listen to me?'

'That's why I'm here,' said Don Camillo, seating him in front of the fire.

'Father, did you see exactly what happened?' the sergeant asked him after a few seconds had gone by.

'Yes, I was just coming out of the tobacconist's, where I had gone to buy some stamps, and I saw the whole thing. I saw you throw yourself in front of the bull and shoot him down.'

The sergeant smiled and shook his head.

'Did you see me shoot *at* him with a pistol and *bring him down* with a machine-gun?'

Don Camillo threw out his arms.

'Sergeant, I'm not an arms expert. I know you had a firearm of some sort in your hand, but I couldn't swear to what it was.'

'Do you mean that you can't tell the difference between a pistol-shot and the crackle of a machine-gun?'

'It's not taught in the seminary, Sergeant.'

'But it's taught at the public schools, I can tell you. And so I can't help knowing that the animal at which I shot my pistol was milled by a volley from a machine-gun.'

'Sergeant, if you say so, I can't contradict you. I repeat, that's not my speciality. The main thing is that the bull was killed before it could gore the life out of you and those poor women who were huddling behind you. I don't see any point in a discussion of ballistics.'

'Yes, the machine-gun volley did save the lives of quite a few people. The only trouble is that it had to come from a machine-gun.'

Don Camillo shrugged his shoulders.

'I'm no expert, as I've said twice before,' he insisted. 'But I may say that what you call a "machine-gun volley" might just as easily have come from a shotgun. I don't see how your higher-ups could find anything wrong with that.'

'If it were just a matter of explaining to the higher-ups, that's a plausible story,' said the sergeant. 'But how am I to justify it to myself? You see, Father, a Carabiniere is never alone; there is always another Carabiniere on watch inside him.'

The Carabiniere touched his breast, and Don Camillo smiled.

'If you were dead, would he be dead too?'

'Exactly. But I'm not dead, and the Carabiniere inside me says: "Someone in the village has a machine-gun, in perfect working order. This is against the law, so you must proceed against him."'

Don Camillo lit and puffed at the butt of his cigar.

'There's no use talking in riddles,' he said. 'Say what you have on your mind. If you suspect me, I am at your disposal. You and your double can proceed against me.'

'Father, let's drop the joking. I know who shot the machine-gun, and so do you, because you saw it.'

'You've come to the wrong place,' said Don Camillo harshly, looking him straight in the eyes. 'I'm the last person in the world to give out such information. And, if you like, you can summon me for failing to cooperate with the law. I haven't another Carabiniere inside me, but I have my conscience, and there is a lot that the both of you could learn from that.'

'There's one thing it couldn't teach us! A private citizen, who is the local leader of a movement in favour of revolution and mob rule, has no right to own a machine-gun!'

'I don't care about revolutions and their local leaders,' said Don Camillo. 'I only want to tell you that I'm neither a spy nor an informer.'

'You've misunderstood me,' said the sergeant, shaking his head. 'I only came to ask you how a honest man can report and turn in someone who has just saved a number of lives, including his own. And how can an honest man *not* report and turn in the owner of a weapon which is a menace to the community?'

Don Camillo was somewhat pacified.

'Sergeant,' he said, 'as you've just put it, the weapon is the menace, not its owner. There's been entirely too much melodrama for strictly political reasons, over machine-guns. They're certainly lethal arms, but not everyone that has one in his possession is a criminal. The owner of a hammer or a kitchen knife may be just as much of a threat to society. When a man has been through the war, his machine-gun may be a sentimental reminder of an honourable past, of days of faith, hope, and self-sacrifice. . . .'

'I see,' the sergeant interrupted. 'Just a well-oiled little souvenir that can fell the biggest bull for miles around!'

'And save the lives of several citizens, including a sergeant of the Carabinieri!'

'Father,' said the sergeant, rising from his chair, 'I can

look, successfully or unsuccessfully, for the machine-gun's owner. But I simply *must* find the gun.'

'You'll find it,' said Don Camillo, rising in his turn to bid his guest good-bye. 'I'll bring it to you myself.'

Once the sergeant had gone, Don Camillo hurried over to the house of Peppone.

'You did a good job, killing the bull,' he told him. 'Now hand over that machine-gun.'

'Are you trying to make me laugh?' asked Peppone.

'Peppone, the sergeant knows that you fired the gun. Even if you saved his life, it's his duty to report you for the possession of a concealed weapon. . . .'

'The sergeant must be mad. He can't know anything of the kind. I don't own a machine-gun, and I never, even in my wildest dreams, killed a bull.'

'Peppone, stop joking. You shot the bull; I saw you with my own eyes.'

'Then go and tell the sergeant. Why come to me?'

'I'm not a spy, I'm a minister of God, and God doesn't need me to tell *Him* anything.'

'You're a minister of the Vatican and the U.S.A.,' Peppone retorted; 'that's why you want to make trouble for honest men.'

Don Camillo had resolved not to let himself be drawn into an argument, and so did not answer, but merely sought to convince Peppone of the gravity of the sergeant's dilemma. But Peppone jeered at all his supplications.

'I don't know what you're talking about,' he said. 'All these machine-guns, bulls, and sergeants have nothing to do with me. You'd better knock at some other door. Better luck next time! You might try the parish priest. See if he doesn't come up with a machine-gun!'

Don Camillo was disconsolate as he left Peppone's house. From the door he fired his parting shot:

'I shan't mind if you're called up by the police. It's no

more than you deserve. But I *am* sorry for the sergeant because he'd never choose to repay you in this fashion for saving his life and the daily bread of his children.'

'Don't worry about me,' sneered Peppone. 'If I'd had this machine-gun you're talking about, I'd have shot the sergeant, not the bull!'

When he got back to the rectory Don Camillo paced restlessly up and down the hall. At last he came to a decision and went precipitately upstairs. The dusty attic was pitch-black, but he needed no light to find what he was looking for. Immediately he located the brick which had only to be pushed at one end to open out at the other. He removed this from the wall and stuck his arm into the opening until his fingers caught hold of a nail with a wire wrapped around it. He unhooked the wire and pulled until a long, narrow box came out of the wall. Then he took out the contents of the box and went to his second-floor bedroom in order to see if it was in good condition. After that he put on his coat and left the house, making his way first through the hedge and then across the open fields. When he came to the area of underbrush near the Canal he waited for midnight to arrive. As the bells rang and fireworks and guns began to pop, he contributed a salvo of his own. Then he made straight for the headquarters of the Carabinieri. The sergeant was still there and Don Camillo said at once:

'Here's what you called a machine-gun. Don't ask me where it came from or who gave it to me.'

'I'm not asking anything,' answered the sergeant. 'I'm simply thanking you for your cooperation, and wishing you a Happy New Year.'

'Happy New Year to you, and to the other Carabiniere inside you!' muttered Don Camillo, wrapping his coat about him and hurrying away.

Ten minutes later the sergeant's doorbell rang again, and when he went to open the door a heavy object which had been leaning up against it fell on to the floor. Attached to it by a wire was a piece of cardboard, on which someone had pasted letters cut out from newspaper headlines. These bore the message: 'A machine-gun guilty of having saved the life of a police *sargint*.'

'By their spelling, ye shall know them,' the sergeant said, laughing to himself.

Then, having laid the object beside the one brought in a few minutes before by Don Camillo, he threw out his arms and exclaimed (contrary, perhaps, to the feelings of Togo, the bull):

'Thanks, all too many thanks, to Saint Anthony Abbot, patron saint of the lost-and-found!'

A Poacher's Penance

DON CAMILLO had planned an epoch-making celebration of the New Year, based on the simple slogan: 'A Chicken in Every Poor Man's Pot'. He started, a fortnight in advance, to take a collection, visiting every landowner and tenant-farmer in his parish and receiving their unanimous approval. Unfortunately, in many barnyards he was told that there had been a round of diseases; in some all the poultry had been sold and those that were left after a penurious autumn were noticeably scrawny. In short, Don Camillo found himself on 30 December with only half a dozen chickens, the fattest among them looking like Smilzo in disguise. Six chickens, when he needed at least thirty! In his distress he went to the crucified Christ on the altar.

'Lord,' he said, 'is it possible for people to be so niggardly? What's one chicken, to a man that has a hundred?'

'It's one chicken, after all,' Christ answered.

Don Camillo threw out his arms in protest.

'Lord,' he went on indignantly, 'how can people fail to make a small sacrifice which would yield them so much joy?'

'Don Camillo, too many people regard any sacrifice as a great one and are entirely wrapped up in seeking their own happiness. To them happiness may mean *not* giving something they don't need.'

'Lord,' said Don Camillo impatiently, between clenched teeth, 'if You know these people so well, why don't You treat them the way they deserve? Why don't You send a frost to freeze the wheat in their fields?'

'Bread belongs to everyone, not merely to the man that sowed the wheat. The land does not bear its fruits only for the benefit of those that own it. It is blasphemy, Don Camillo, to ask the Lord to freeze the wheat in the ground. Don't we all say: "Give us this day our daily bread"?'

'Forgive me,' said Don Camillo, bowing his head. 'I only meant that certain selfish people aren't fit to own land.'

'If they had sown stones instead of wheat, then they wouldn't be entitled to any reward. But if they raise what it is proper for the land to bear, then they are entitled to own and run it their own way.'

Don Camillo lost patience altogether.

'Lord,' he said, 'You're on the side of the land-owners!'

'No,' said Christ with a smile: 'My interest is in the land itself. . . . Once upon a time there was an island, inhabited by very poor people. There were two doctors on the island, one generous, the other grasping. The first doctor asked very small fees, but unfortunately he was less skilled in his art than the other. And all the sick flocked to the more competent man. Was this fair?'

Don Camillo shrugged his shoulders.

'It was only normal that they should go to a doctor who could cure them. But I can't accept the fact that a good man should be in need, while a bad one should be making money. That isn't just.'

'It isn't just, Don Camillo, but it's human. It's human that sick people should pay heavy fees to the abler of the two. On the other hand, it's just that God should punish him for abusing his God-given talents.'

'Lord,' insisted Don Camillo, 'I . . .'

'If you lived on the island in question, would you ask God to destroy the competent doctor and preserve the inept one?'

'No,' said Don Camillo, 'I'd ask Him to teach the competent man to be generous and the generous man to improve his skill.'

'Well, isn't a farmer a kind of doctor responsible for the health and prosperity of the land?'

'Lord,' Don Camillo explained, 'I understand now, and beg God to forgive my foolish words. But I can't help worrying about the fact that I need thirty chickens and have no more than six in hand.'

'Eight,' Christ corrected him.

'Yes, eight,' said Don Camillo, who had forgotten the fact that there were two capons in his own yard.

It's no easy job to find twenty-two chickens from one day to the next. Don Camillo knew this perfectly well, because he had searched a fortnight for half a dozen. But he had no intention of falling down on his slogan, 'A Chicken in Every Poor Man's Pot'.

He was eating out his soul for an answer, when suddenly another question rose before him.

'Yes, a chicken's just a chicken. But what is a pheasant?'

To be logical, a pheasant is a pheasant. But is it necessary to be so precise? Couldn't a pheasant be called a 'flying chicken'? He concluded that the celebration would be the same with the slogan of 'A Pheasant in Every Poor Man's Frying-pan'. There were only two drawbacks to this variant. First, the question of finding twenty-two pheasants, and second, the lack of time for them to season. Don Camillo walked for miles up and down the rectory hall, debating these problems. Finally he resolved them by a further modification of the original slogan. Now it was 'A Pheasant in Every Poor Man's Shopping Bag'. All the essentials were there.

Don Camillo's dog, Thunder, agreed that the main thing was to find twenty-two pheasants to replace the missing chickens. He found it quite natural that his master should don a pair of trousers, a corduroy jacket, and a cyclist's cap. It wasn't the first time that Don Camillo had gone hunting in places where a cassock would have been in the way. What was unnatural was that Don Camillo should go out of the house without his shotgun over his shoulder. The dog felt sure that it was a lapse of memory, and just as the priest was about to step through the garden he barked at him to return to the house. When they were back in the dining-room, Thunder looked up at the gun and cartridge-belt and game-bag that were hanging on the wall.

'Come on, Thunder!' ordered Don Camillo.

'Take your gun, and then I'll come,' Thunder answered, without moving. He said all this by barking, but it was perfectly understandable to Don Camillo.

'Stop that noise, and come along,' the priest answered. 'The shotgun's staying there. We can't possibly take such a noisy weapon.'

Then, when Thunder remained obstinately still, Don Camillo dug into the left leg of his trousers and came up with a single-barrelled gun. Thunder looked at it in a puzzled fashion and compared it with the gun hanging on the wall.

'That isn't a shotgun,' he said at last. 'The shotgun's up there.'

Don Camillo knew that Thunder's pedigree lent him a

certain dignity and entitled him to be treated with respect.

'This is a shotgun, too,' he explained. 'A small, old-fashioned model, with the charger on the barrel. It's not very powerful, of course, but if you shoot at a distance of two or three yards at a silly pheasant it will bring him down.'

He gave a demonstration of how to load it and then, opening the window over the garden he aimed at a tin can which someone had mounted on the end of a pole. The gun gave a faint click, and the can hit the dust. Thunder ran downstairs to follow up the prey. Soon he called back:

'Let's go hunting for tin cans, then, if you insist!'

The pheasants perched lethargically on the lowest branches of the trees. For three years the Finetti family had lived abroad, and in all that time no one had fired a shot on their preserve. The pheasants were so fat and self-confident that it was hardly necessary to shoot them; they could have just as easily been swept up in the crown of a hat. Nevertheless, Don Camillo chose to use his gun. Every time the gun clicked a pheasant fell to the ground. Although he had to waste considerable time searching for the bodies, Don Camillo bagged twenty-one pheasants without the least trouble. But the twenty-second was appointed by fate to give him trouble.

Thunder was showing signs of restlessness, and this signified the presence of something other than pheasants and rabbits. But Don Camillo was so intent on bagging the twenty-second 'flying chicken' that he told the dog to be quiet and let him get on with the job. Thunder unwillingly obeyed until, just as Don Camillo was shooting his intended victim, he really barked an alarm. It was too late, because the game warden was already near. Don Camillo threw his gun into the bushes, and picking up the bag that contained the twenty-one pheasants, he ran off on the double. Evening was starting to fall and a thick fog mercifully interposed itself between Don Camillo and his pursuer. Thunder masterfully led the strategic withdrawal, and having found a hole in the high wire fence around the preserve he stood by it until Don Camillo had passed through.

Don Camillo was of elephantine proportions and the bagful of pheasants was quite bulky, but he dived into the fence with all the ardour of a goalkeeper in a soccer game. The warden arrived only in time to see Don Camillo's hindquarters disappearing through the fence. He shot at them, without much hope of hitting the mark. A few minutes later Don Camillo emerged on to the road. He couldn't cut across the fields because just opposite the fence there was the eight-feet wide canal, swollen with water. The road was the only way he could go, and here the warden would surely have found him, because it ran parallel to the fence for half a mile in either direction.

'Home, Thunder!' he shouted to the dog, who set out immediately in the right direction, while he himself continued to run. 'He's not going to identify me, even if I have to throw myself into the canal,' he muttered to himself.

At the curve of the Wayside Shrine, Don Camillo saw a big truck coming down the road. He stood on the ridge along the Canal and waved his cap. Then, without waiting for the truck to stop, he jumped on to the running-board. The driver wore a concerned expression as he jammed on the brakes. Within a second Don Camillo had opened the door and installed himself in the cab.

'Keep going, man, for the love of God!' he shouted.

The driver depressed the clutch, and the truck regained speed as if someone had kicked it in the rear. After half a mile or so, the driver mumbled:

'I took you for a gunman. Why, in heaven's name, are you in such a hurry?'

'I've got to make the six-twenty-two train.'

'Oh, you are a wild-fowl fancier, are you?'

'No, I sell detergents for washing black souls.'

'I was a fool,' said the driver. 'I should never have picked you up, and then the game warden would have seen your typically Vatican-agent face. Well, I must admit that you've done things in a big way. Are you expecting a lot of people to dinner?'

'Yes, thirty. I had two chickens and people gave me six more. After that, I had to find twenty-two birds of some other kind, in order that there should be one for every neighbour of ours that couldn't afford it. I had just taken aim at the twenty-second when the game warden saw me. That's the whole story. Do you need any more data to report to your Party?'

'All I need is some idea as to what is your moral code.'

'That of a good Christian and an honest citizen.'

'Then, Mister Priest, let's take a look at the past,' said Peppone, slowing the truck down. 'Last month, when I suggested that we make common cause to procure firewood for the unemployed, you wouldn't hear of it; in fact you fought me all along the line. Why was that?'

'Because I couldn't encourage people to break the law,' said Don Camillo, lighting the butt of his cigar.

'What law?'

'The law for the protection of private property. The poor have a right to firewood, there I agree. But one can't say to them: "Let's go and take it from the rich landowners!" "Thou shalt not steal" is the law of both God and man.'

' "Thou shalt not steal," is that it?' shouted Peppone. 'If workers can't touch the property of the rich, what right have the rich to rob the workers of a decent wage and thus make it impossible for them to go on living?'

'It's no use your haranguing me as if I were at a political rally,' expostulated Don Camillo. 'I can't help anyone to break the law.'

'Very well,' said Peppone. 'Then let's look at the chapter you've just written. The poor have a right to a good New Year's Day dinner, but the rich won't give it to them. So what does the priest do? He breaks the law of God and man by stealing pheasants from a private hunting preserve. Do priests have a moral code all their own, or have they a right to violate the so-called public law with impunity?'

'Comrade, I claim no such right. I took off my priestly garb and disguised myself in order to break the law without attracting attention to my person. But last month I couldn't parade through the streets, arm in arm with our comrade mayor, shouting: "The law is unjust! Down with the law! We're taking the law into our own hands!..." If I am a soldier parading before a general, I have to salute him; if I don't want to do it, then I must get out of the parade. The one thing I can't do is parade in front of him with my hands in my pockets, shouting: "I'm not saluting any such no-good general as you!..." Yes, I did steal the pheasants. But I didn't call out: "Come on, Comrades; the pheasants are ours!"'

Peppone shook his head and pounded with one fist on the steering-wheel.

'You preach against stealing, and then you steal!' he objected. 'Your preaching is one thing, and your practice another.'

'According to your standards, Peppone, I preach what's wrong and practise what's right. But I still maintain that the opposite is true. If I tell people the right thing, then I am doing them good. And if then I go and do something wrong, quite off my own bat, I'm wronging only myself. Of course, I must answer for my wrongdoing and be punished for it. I may elude human justice, but God's justice will catch up with me, sooner or later.'

'That's a convenient way to look at it,' sneered Peppone. 'You allow yourself to get away with practically anything in this world, by saying that you'll pay for it in the next. I say that you ought to pay up on the spot!'

'Don't worry; I'll pay soon enough, because my conscience will prick me. As a good Christian and an honest citizen, I'm aware of having violated the law of both God and man.'

'Hmmm . . .' said Peppone. 'I tell you where that Christian and civic conscience of yours is – it's at the . . . base of your spine!'

'Very well, Peppone,' said Don Camillo, with a sigh. 'Granted that my conscience is located where you say, does that have any effect on what I have just told you?'

'What are you driving at now, Father?' asked Peppone disgustedly.

'Nothing so very deep. I'd just like to know, Comrade, whether you've ever had a bullet in the base of your spine?'

Don Camillo's voice seemed to come from very far away, and when Peppone switched on the light on the dashboard he saw that the priest was deathly pale.

'Father! . . .' he gasped.

'Put out that light, and don't worry,' said Don Camillo. 'It's just a little prick of my conscience, and I'll get over it. Take me to the old doctor at Torricella; he'll take the lead out of my pants without asking any questions.'

Peppone drove as if he were jet propelled over the bumpy road and put Don Camillo down at the doctor's door. While he was waiting for him to come out he wiped the blood off the seat. Then he hid the bag of pheasants below it and went for a stroll in the course of which he had ample time for meditation. An hour later Don Camillo emerged from the doctor's house.

'How goes it?' asked Peppone.

'Well, my conscience is at rest, in a manner of speaking, but for spiny or spinal reasons I must admit that I'm better off in a standing than in a sitting position. If you don't object, I'll stand in the rear of the truck, and mind you don't go too fast!'

Fortunately the rear of the truck had a canvas cover, so that Don Camillo did not suffer too much from the wind. The fog was thicker than ever and so he was able to slip into the rectory unnoticed, followed by Peppone, carrying the bag of birds, which he deposited in the cellar. When Peppone came upstairs he found Don Camillo back in his priestly uniform. The black cassock made his face look all the whiter.

'Father,' he muttered, 'if there's anything I can do for you, don't hesitate to call on me.'

'I'm quite all right,' said Don Camillo, 'but I'm worried about Thunder. See if you can find him.'

There came a whimper from under the table, which was Thunder's way of answering 'Present!' to the mention of his name. Peppone bent over to look at him more closely.

'It seems as if his . . . conscience were bothering him too,' said Peppone. 'Shall I take him to the same discreet doctor?'

'No,' said Don Camillo. 'This is a strictly family affair. Carry him up to my bedroom and I'll operate on him myself.'

Thunder allowed Peppone to carry him up to the second floor. When Peppone came down he stood at the door, with one finger pointing to heaven, and looked severely at Don Camillo.

'The sins of the priests are visited upon the innocent dogs,' he observed sententiously.

'Not fair!' retorted Don Camillo. 'The priest in question is half-dead!' He was still standing on his two feet and still looking very pale.

When Peppone had gone he barred the front door and went down to the cellar to look at the twenty-one 'flying chickens'. There turned out to be twenty-two of them, because while he was waiting for Don Camillo to come out of the doctor's Peppone had bought a magnificent capon. Before Don Camillo went to throw himself (face down) on his bed, he went to kneel before the crucified Christ on the altar.

'Lord,' he said, 'I can't thank You for having protected me, because I was doing a dishonest deed and one that deserved to be punished. Perhaps the game warden's shotgun ought to have dispatched me to the next world.'

'Even the worst of priests is worth more than twenty-two pheasants,' answered Christ severely.

'Twenty-one, to be exact,' whispered Don Camillo, 'I'm not responsible for the twenty-second.'

'You meant to shoot him down, however.'

'Lord, my heart is very sore, because I know that I have done wrong.'

'You're lying, Don Camillo. Your heart is full of joy, because you're thinking of the happiness coming to thirty needy families tomorrow.'

Don Camillo rose, stepped back, and sat heavily down in the first pew. Perspiration trickled down his increasingly pale face.

'Rise!' said the crucified Christ. '*Ego te absolvo*. Your sins are forgiven.'

An Exchange of Courtesies

'THE only way to have a genuine exchange of courtesies with the Catholic workers is to belabour them with a stick. But directives are directives, and so we'll simply tickle them with a feather.'

These were Peppone's words to his lieutenants, and he accompanied them with the observation that talk is all very well, but that to get anything concrete accomplished by workers – Catholic or non-Catholic – you must begin by subtracting something from their wallets.

'When the priest is in the pulpit, he's unbeatable,' Peppone went on. 'If he has nothing better to say, he can always fall back on dogma, the Ten Commandments, Heaven, Hell, and all the rest. But when he stands behind the counter of the Co-operative Store, then his authority is not the same. There's where we must attack him.'

For a long time the 'People's Co-operative' had been a thorn in Don Camillo's side, a thorn whose sting even the 'White Co-operative' of his own creation could not remove, because the Reds dealt not only in food and other articles but they had also a bar, a tobacco shelf, a television set, and petrol pump. Altogether it was big business and functioned very smoothly; he knew that he would never be able to transform his frail enterprise into one equally powerful. He ate his heart out continuously, and every time he was told something new about the Red Co-operative he felt as if he had taken a beating.

As soon as the plan for 'an exchange of courtesies' was put into action, Don Camillo's beating was worse than ever. For one day the Reds lowered the price of bacon, another the price of cheese, the next oil and so on. Soon Camillo could not compete with these crazy reductions and so he simply tried to stop up as many holes as he could and stay afloat. He was hardened by now to adversity and when he felt especially low in his mind and sought the succour of the Christ on the main altar, he simply threw out his arms disconsolately and said:

'Lord, You see how things are. I don't ask You to take an interest in my paltry shop, but I do beg You to help me keep my temper.'

God did help him and he achieved considerable self-control, but when he heard about the new department in their Co-operative store his temper boiled up within him. He was not satisfied with other people's description and went to see for himself. The window which had formerly served to show groceries was now given over to the new merchandise, and a big sign explained that in order to meet its customers' every want the Co-operative had undertaken to sell materials and patterns for making baptismal, First Communion, and wedding outfits, not to mention handsomely decorated candles. 'Compare prices,' said the sign, 'and see who is exploiting the religious feelings of good Catholic workers.' This sign was set up in the middle of the display, at the feet of a big statue of Saint Joseph the Worker, while another sign, nearby, explained that the 'People's Co-operative' also furnished printed invitations to any of the above functions, with a wide variety of conventional texts.

As if by chance, Smilzo appeared at the Co-operative door and whispered into Don Camillo's ear:

'Father, you'd better get some of those candles. We give a fifteen per cent discount to active clergy. That means we lose money, but what does it matter? We want to help the Church.'

There was a small crowd in front of the window, and Don Camillo could not afford to lose his temper. All he could do was seize the peak of Smilzo's cap between the thumb and forefinger of his left hand and pull it down all the way to the chin. But Smilzo managed to have the last word.

'Nothing doing, Father!' he exclaimed from under his cap. 'The Dark Ages are over!'

The next morning Don Camillo found three handsomely decorated votive candles burning in the Lady Chapel. The day after there were six, and it was quite obvious that the Reds had put them there, simply to annoy him. In order to be certain he hid in a confessional, and sure enough, that very afternoon an elderly man came into the church, crossed himself and made resolutely for Saint Anthony's chapel. From underneath his coat he extracted one of the famous candles, which he proceeded to light and then to fit into a holder. It was just at this moment that Don Camillo appeared at his side. To the priest's amazement, the fellow was not a Red but one of his own faithful, Matteo Frossi by name.

'Matteo,' exclaimed Don Camillo; 'I'd never have expected *you* to play a filthy trick like that!'

'Is it a filthy trick to light a candle to Saint Anthony?' asked the astonished old man.

'It's a filthy trick to light one of *those* candles, and you know it!'

'Father, if I can give thanks to Saint Anthony and save thirty liras at the same time, why should you object?

The wax of this candle and the wax of yours come from the same place!'

After Frossi had gone away, Don Camillo gave vent to his feelings before the crucified Christ on the main altar.

'The human race is growing cheaper and cheaper, Lord,' he told Him. 'Judas sold You for thirty pieces of silver, but this fellow sells You for thirty miserable liras!'

'Who are you talking about, Don Camillo?'

'This fellow, Frossi, who just lit a candle to Saint Anthony.'

'Don Camillo, didn't you promise never to drag me into the affairs of your paltry shop? Have you lost your memory?'

'No, Lord; I've lost my temper.' And Don Camillo humbly bowed his head.

Eventually, although it cost him a considerable effort, Don Camillo regained his composure. In the pulpit and out of it he said what he thought he should about the ridiculous tactics with which certain people tried to deceive the faithful. He explained that Satan employs the most devious means to win men's souls, and that, like the Greeks, he is most to be feared when he brings gifts. For every apparent gift, Satan extracts a hundredfold return; he exploits our sloth and our avarice together.

Certainly Don Camillo himself didn't play Satan's game. Rather than buy it at the 'People's Co-operative', he ate a whole meal one day without salt, and one rainy night he rode eight miles on his bicycle in order to purchase a cigar at Torricella. This was the least of what he was willing to do for the sake of boycotting Peppone. He was called upon to make the supreme sacrifice the day when he went to collect donations for the Orphan Asylum. As usual, he borrowed a truck from Filotti and with the aid of a husky boy picked up produce from all the neighbouring farms. When the truck was filled with wheat, maize, potatoes, apples, and wood he drove happily back to the village. The motor had worked like a dream, the farmers had given cheerfully, and it was a mild, sunny day. He turned down the main street of the village, which went by the 'People's Co-operative' and then, two hundred yards farther on, to the square in front of the church. Just thirty yards from the 'People's Co-operative' the engine began to sputter. It seemed as if Satan himself must have had a hand in the matter, for it came to a stop in front of the petrol pump. Don Camillo got out, opened the hood, and then went round to take the cap off the tank.

'We're out of fuel,' he told his helper.

'Well, we're pretty lucky,' said the boy gaily. 'There's the pump, right beside us.'

A roar from Don Camillo compelled him to silence. But the enemy was already in the know. The enemy was standing at the door of the Co-operative, enjoying the autumn sun. And he had not only keen hearing but also knew a lot about engines.

'Good evening, Father,' he said amiably.

'Good evening, Mr Mayor,' Don Camillo answered between clenched teeth, and turned to talk to the boy.

A minute later the entire group of Peppone's lieutenants and a large number of his followers poured out of the door and stood round their leader.

'What's up, Chief?' asked Smilzo.

'He's out of fuel,' answered Peppone.

'Too bad it didn't happen out in the country,' said Smilzo. 'Here, for just over a hundred liras, he can get enough to take him home.'

'You mean to say he'd have the nerve to buy no more than a quart?' muttered Bigio.

'He's just as likely to ask for a pint,' Smilzo answered, with a mocking laugh. 'You don't know how tough and stingy these priests can be.'

They talked among themselves, turning their backs to Don Camillo, but in such loud voices that they could be heard all the way to the edge of the village. It was only natural that Don Camillo's temper should rise to boiling-point, but he held it in and continued to confer, from the place where he was standing, with the boy in the seat of the truck. At this point Peppone entered his henchmen's discussion.

'A pint, did you say? He can't use a single drop of it. This is the devil's own petrol, and if he were to take so much as a teaspoonful the Standard Oil Company would excommunicate him.'

'Then what's he going to do, Chief?' Smilzo asked.

'That's easy,' said Peppone to the small crowd which had gathered about him. 'Priests' cars have two fuelling systems: one of them runs on petrol and the other on prayers. He'll fill the tank with Our Fathers, press the starter, and the Holy Ghost will ignite the motor.'

They all laughed. At this Don Camillo couldn't resist looking them in the face and saying what was on his mind. Swelling up his chest and shaking his fist in the direction of Peppone, he said:

'You can leave the Holy Ghost out of it. I'll manage alone.'

'That's what you think,' Smilzo retorted. 'But a Don Camillo won't do; it will take a Don Caterpillar!'

Don Camillo lost control of himself altogether.

'Hold the wheel!' he shouted to the boy, leaping to the rear of the truck and pushing on it.

Something creaked: either Don Camillo's bones, or the rear of the truck, perhaps both of them together. Don Camillo was no longer a man, he was a living jack. Peppone's gang was breathless, for one of two things was bound to happen: either the truck would move or Don Camillo would break into small pieces. With God's help, the truck moved slowly ahead. Peppone's gang paraded after it, in horror and fascination. After fifty yards Don

Camillo had to catch his breath. He stood up straight and turned around:

'If four of you big oafs are capable of doing what I did alone, let them step forward,' he said.

Naturally no four of them moved; only the massive Peppone solemnly answered the challenge. He signalled to Don Camillo to get out of the way and applied his shoulder to the rear of the truck. Once more there was a creaking sound; once more nothing broke and the truck moved slowly ahead. Ten, twenty, thirty, forty, fifty yards, but Peppone did not stop even when he had reached a hundred. As the truck rolled down the street the Reds exulted; they broke into loud shouts and soon the street was filled with people. Peppone was like a powerful traction-belt; he went on to a hundred and ten, a hundred and twenty yards, and finally all the way to the church square, where the crowd thunderously applauded him. Don Camillo did not bat an eyelash; he waited until Peppone had stopped panting and the applause had subsided. Then he raised his arms to ask for silence.

'Good enough,' he observed. 'I was looking for some sucker to push the truck all the way home for nothing.'

'I'm not so much of a sucker as you may think,' shouted Peppone.

His henchmen caught the idea. Smilzo edged the boy out of the seat and took the wheel; the others hurled themselves at the front of the car and pushed it all the way back to the petrol pump. There they stopped, and when Don Camillo re-joined them Peppone had his say.

'He who laughs last laughs best. The rectory is still two hundred yards away. Go to it, Father!'

Don Camillo kept cool and lit the butt of his cigar.

'Will you have some petrol, Father?' asked Smilzo, going over to the pump.

'Thanks, I've got some,' said Don Camillo, climbing on to the seat, opening the emergency valve and pressing the starter. Under its own power the truck went triumphantly back to the church square. Peppone's gang looked on with their mouths hanging wide open, until their leader threw his cap on the ground and began to protest:

'That's the second time he's fooled me with his emergency valve!'

But Smilzo had something more to say:

'Chief, you did a hundred and fifty yards to his fifty. You lost one to three, and saved your honour.'

Thus they sought to find what consolation they could in writing an end to the story. But people still talk about it and bid fair to go on talking.

A Speech to Go Down in History

'FOR that meeting on the twenty-sixth, we've got to think up something special,' Peppone said gravely.

Bigio, Brusco, and Smilzo all looked puzzled, and Peppone hastened to enlighten them.

'We're lucky enough to have our rally scheduled as the last one before the election, which means that no matter what we say no one can contradict it. But we're called upon for some substantial oratory, not just the usual hot air. There's no question of bringing in a speaker from the outside, because this is a local election, and we're on our own. We've got to produce something smashing, something that will go down in history.'

His three aides relaxed. If this was all he had on his mind, there was no need to worry.

'Chief, we're riding the crest of the wave,' Smilzo answered gaily. 'All you have to do is drive the last nail in their coffin!'

Peppone shook his head.

'A concluding speech is no joke. Election eve is not the time for a political harangue. It's got to be something factual: a record of past accomplishments and a pledge of others to come. It's one thing to promise social justice, and another to date the opening of a public laundry. Big ideas are all very well for a national election, but on the local level it's better to stick to the concrete. The question is how to make parish-pump politics sound epoch-making.'

Smilzo continued to dissent.

'If a fellow knows what he wants to say, it's simple enough to say it.'

'Simple, indeed!' retorted Peppone. 'But one point I grant you. It's a question not of just the appropriate thing, but of what you *want* to say. An historical speech can't be improvised; it must be thought out in advance, with every word weighed and every effect calculated. Words aren't enough; you've got to know their meanings. It takes spadework with the dictionary.'

'You have a big enough vocabulary, Chief,' Smilzo assured him. 'Why work so hard over it?'

'A big vocabulary isn't enough, I tell you,' shouted Peppone. 'I need peace and quiet, for purposes of meditation. That's why I've called you together. Even if the People's Palace goes up in smoke, or Togliatti himself makes a tour of inspection, yes, even come the revolution, I'm not to be disturbed. No one must break the continuity of my speech. Have I made myself clear?'

They understood him perfectly.

'Chief,' said Smilzo, 'even if we have to guard your house with machine-guns, no one shall come near you. Just leave it to us!'

This is why, at a certain point, Peppone disappeared from circulation.

Just as election day was drawing close and the atmosphere was growing hotter and hotter, when his enemies were showing their claws and a strong hand was needed to put them in their place, Peppone vanished from sight. Had he been taken ill? Purged? Gone underground? Sent on a secret mission? His workshop was silent and the sign hanging on the door carried the simple word 'Closed'. The windows and doors of his own house were barred and his children were staying at their grandmother's, with not a word to be got out of them. Even his wife was gone.

Don Camillo sent out spies and alerted all the gossipy old women of the village. He himself walked by Peppone's house, but found no clue to the mystery. But in a village so small that everyone knew everything about his neighbour, such a situation could not long endure. News leaked through to the rectory that Peppone's house was not deserted, that his wife had been seen at the window and every night Smilzo delivered a parcel there and then came home empty-handed. Smilzo was tailed and found to be going every day to buy food at Castelletto, food sufficient to fill two hungry mouths. When it was discovered that Smilzo also bought cigars, then it was obvious that although one of the mouths might belong to Peppone's wife, the other indubitably belonged to Peppone. Decoys dogged Smilzo's footsteps, and one evening he let them treat him to too many glasses of sparkling red *lambrusco* wine. They brought up the subject of politics and remarked how strange it was that Peppone should be absent from the scene. One of the decoys said argumentatively:

'There's nothing so strange about it. It's a bad case of yellow liver. He knows the game is up and doesn't dare show his face.'

'Just wait till you hear his historical speech, after all the work he's putting into it!' said Smilzo, falling like a ton of bricks for their little game.

Five minutes later Don Camillo was informed, but the news did not disturb him.

'Is that all?' he puffed. 'Not worth talking about!'

And indeed he did not bring up the subject again. But that very night an unknown hand wrote on Peppone's door:

Here lies Comrade Giuseppe Bottazzi,
Who has sought solitude
In order to write an historical election-eve oration.
The question is whether, when it's written,
He'll know how to read it.

Although Don Camillo had dismissed the matter as unworthy of mention, this epigraph caused all malicious tongues to wag about it. Such tongues are not too numerous in the Po valley, or at least there is no more than one to every inhabitant, and not the six or seven which seem to be the sources of so vast a volume of gossip.

Meanwhile the blissfully ignorant Peppone continued to toil over his epoch-making speech. His faithful and discreet wife moved about the house in bedroom slippers in order not to break its continuity. Peppone had never worked so hard in all his life. He worked as hard as if he were forging a hundred-foot iron fence, complete with an ornate gate. The stakes were high. His enemies were dead set on getting into power, whereas Peppone and his gang sought their third consecutive re-election. What with weighing every word and polishing every sentence, Peppone expended far more time than he had imagined, and the final touches were added no earlier than the Friday morning before the historical Saturday night. Then, oddly enough, the scribbler's prophecy was fulfilled, and Peppone was unable to read what he had written. Fortunately, this possibility had been taken into consideration. Smilzo had been standing by for two days, and now he took over the precious manuscript, jumped on to his motor-cycle, and rode madly to the city, where a loyal typist proceeded to tap out two copies, one for Peppone and the other for . . . history.

It was late at night and Don Camillo was about to go to bed when Caroline, a poor old creature that went about collecting wood and stale bread, brought him a cardboard folder.

'I found it on the edge of a ditch down near *La Piop-pàccia*,' she told him. 'It's full of papers and they may be important to someone. Can you say something about it in church and see if there are any claimants?'

After she had gone away Don Camillo examined the papers. Soon he realized, to his amazement, that he had Peppone's historical speech in hand, the original and two copies.

Meanwhile Smilzo was sitting under a poplar on the river bank, with death in his heart. He had lost the folder containing the speech. It had slipped out of his pocket while he was riding home, full speed, from the city. Twice he had retraced a portion of the route, vainly searching, and then he had sat down to nurse his despair.

'If I come back empty-handed, the chief will kill me,' he said to himself over and over.

And he was not far from right.

Peppone spent an agonizing night. After waiting and waiting for Smilzo to come, he put in a long-distance telephone call. The typist told him that Smilzo had left four hours before, with the masterpiece under his arm. Then he called his general staff, and they sent out search-parties. At four o'clock in the morning, there was still no news of Smilzo, and Peppone, who had been angrily pacing up and down the hall, suddenly collapsed.

'Traitor!' he exclaimed, and let himself be carried off to bed, where he fell into a leaden sleep, accompanied by a high fever.

Smilzo turned up at Bigio's house at nine o'clock. When Bigio heard that the speech was lost he was speechless with dismay. He stared hard at Smilzo and said:

'You may as well emigrate to Venezuela.'

New orders were sent out to the search-parties. They were to stop looking for Smilzo and watch out for a yellow folder which the miserable fellow had lost on the road. A large-scale manoeuvre of this kind could not escape attention. People took note, asked questions, gossiped, put two and two together, and came, by afternoon, to this conclusion: the text of Peppone's famous speech was lost and that evening he would find himself in exceedingly hot water. Which meant that a large crowd would gather to see him squirm.

The meeting was to start at nine o'clock, and by half past eight the square was full. At this last minute Peppone's henchmen collected their courage and went to wake him. They had quite a job to get him even to open his eyes. He was still feverish and his eyelids were leaden. They explained that a huge crowd had gathered in the square and he must make up his mind what to do.

'How about Smilzo?' Peppone asked in a dim faraway voice.

'He's found,' said Bigio.

'And the speech?' Peppone panted.

'It's lost,' said Bigio, prudently retreating three steps.

But he need not have been so cautious. Peppone was too far gone to be a menace. He simply closed his eyes and sighed.

'Chief, what are we going to do?' asked Bigio anxiously.

'Go to the devil, the lot of you,' murmured Peppone, as if in a dream.

'What about the crowd? And the Party?'

'Devil take the crowd and the Party too,' said Peppone pacifically.

His henchmen stared at one another. This was the end.

'There's nothing we can do,' said Bigio. 'We'll have to tell the crowd that the meeting is adjourned because the speaker is ill.'

Just then Don Camillo appeared upon the scene. Obviously he did not expect to find Peppone so stricken, and he looked down in bewilderment at the inert form on the bed. He did not say a word or make his presence felt in any way, but in a few moments Peppone opened first one eye and then the other.

'I'm not ready yet for Extreme Unction,' he muttered.

'Too bad,' said Don Camillo.

'You can go; I don't need you.'

'You always need me, Comrade!' said Don Camillo, taking a big yellow folder out of his pocket and throwing it on to the bed. Peppone reached out, opened it and stared at the contents.

'Check it, now, Comrade,' said Don Camillo, with a laugh. 'Everything's there: the original manuscript and two copies. Remember that "incontrovertible" takes only one *b* and be thankful to your parish priest.'

Peppone slowly slipped the papers back into the folder and hoisted himself into a sitting position. Then he clenched his teeth, looked into Don Camillo's eyes, and said brusquely:

'I'd rather not thank him.'

Peppone's hands were as big as shovels. With a single gesture he ripped the folder and its contents in two, then, as if he were prey to some uncontrollable madness, he tore both pieces into shreds, rolled them up in a ball and threw them out of the window. Next, he leaped out of bed.

It was nine o'clock, and the crowd in the square was beginning to murmur, when suddenly Peppone walked on to the platform. His fever had fallen, or rather it was not the same sort of fever. This was clear at once from the way he said: 'Fellow-citizens! . . .' The crowd was silent and Peppone spoke. He improvised; a dozen times he said 'ain't' and 'don't' for 'isn't' and 'doesn't'; he referred to the 'Nemesis of history' and the 'Nemesis of geography', but the most awkward phrases quite plainly came from a full heart, so that even his severest critics had to admit that he was a good fellow.

So it was that Smilzo didn't emigrate to Venezuela and Peppone was re-elected mayor, without having to thank Don Camillo, but indebted, none the less, to Divine Providence for preventing him from pronouncing a speech that would have gone down in history as abysmally stupid. And Don Camillo was not too perturbed by the outcome of the election, for he knew that in politics we can often obtain more from our enemies than from our friends.

The War of the Carnations

THIS is a commonplace sort of love-story, which
had an unexpected ending on the main square of
the village, to be exact, near one of the low stone
columns which divide this square from the smaller
one in front of the church. There were a large number
of witnesses, because the main square was occupied by
the May-Day celebration of Peppone and his gang,
wearing red carnations in their buttonholes, and the
church square by the white-carnationed followers of
Don Camillo.

In some broken-down shacks in the Po River valley
there are still to be found cheap prints of an old religious
painting which shows Jesus and Saint Joseph, clad in
unmistakably red garments, working at a carpenter's
bench. This was quite a find, from a political point of
view, and it was taken up, at one time, by the old-line
socialists. Long after they had abandoned it, the repre-
sentation of Christ and Saint Joseph as workers and
craftsmen was re-introduced as the theme of a May the
First Catholic Labour Day.

The final episode of our little love-story took place on

the first of these new-style holidays, celebrated on adjacent squares by the conflicting Red and White parties. It was a cool Spring morning, but political temperature was boiling over.

Among the most active members of the White team was Gilda Marossi, an exceedingly pretty young girl, whose political ardour was as great as that of two men put together. And among Peppone's most active henchmen was Angiolino Grisotti, nicknamed Gioli, a heavy-handed sort, who if he hadn't been such a violent Red might have passed for a normal, handsome fellow. The story wouldn't be so commonplace if the two had never met. But they did meet, when they were mere schoolchildren and politics was a complete mystery to them. They met several times after that, too, upon various festive occasions, when they had some notion of what politics was about, but cared more for dancing. Then, when they were in politics up to the ears and discovered that they were sworn enemies, they began to avoid such meetings. One day, however, they found themselves face to face on a bus. For a time they tried to outstare each other, but finally Gilda could hold her peace no longer and said brusquely:

'If some people had the least bit of self-respect they wouldn't stare at their betters.'

'Just what I was thinking, myself,' said Gioli.

Having said all they had to say, they continued to exchange lowering glances all the way to their destination. In spite of their mutual disdain, it was obvious that she was prettier than ever and that in spite of his association with the Reds he was a strikingly handsome fellow. When the bus reached the city, they went their own ways, but a few minutes later Gioli could have kicked himself for his stupidity. He had taken courses in propaganda technique, sponsored by the Party, and now he realized that he had muffed the chance to use an old friendship either to make a convert or to gain insight into the tactics of the enemy. In order to wipe out this error he hatched a new plan.

'A good Communist,' he said to himself, 'must be a psychologist as well. And what does psychology say? It says that a girl who takes a bus to the city must be going shopping. She won't go into the first shop she sees, no, not she; she'll look into a dozen windows and compare qualities and prices before she buys a single thing. After wasting so much time window-shopping, she'll be dead tired and just manage to catch the last bus home. That's where I come in. . . .'

And so Angiolino Grisotti, nicknamed Gioli, was one of the first to arrive at the last bus, where he put down a parcel on the seat facing him and patiently waited. According to the dictates of psychology, Gilda should have been the last to arrive and have found every seat except the one which he had reserved for her taken. Unfortunately, she arrived shortly after Gioli, and when he saw her coming he turned pale. When Gilda got on the bus, she could have sat anywhere she pleased, but psychological considerations made her set her mind upon the seat occupied by Gioli's parcel.

'Is this place taken?' she asked firmly, tossing her head in the parcel's direction.

He picked up the parcel and she sat down. They sat stiffly, face to face, for several minutes, until Gioli was inspired to take out a packet of cigarettes and offer one to the silent figure across the way.

'*We* don't smoke in public places,' said Gilda coldly. '*Your* girls do practically anything, either in public or in private, but *we*'ve been taught better.'

'Let's leave politics out of it,' said Gioli, putting the cigarettes back in his pocket. 'Why not talk about you and me?'

'What do you mean by "talk"?' queried Gilda aggressively.

'I mean the way we used to talk when we went dancing together.'

'Only a godless Communist would have the nerve to throw a woman's past weaknesses in her face,' said Gilda stiffly. 'Why don't you print on one of your posters that for a while I lent an ear to your foolishness?'

'Why should I?' asked Gioli. 'This is a personal matter, not a Party one. Of course, if you can't talk to me for fear of offending the fiancé whom the parish priest has forced upon you, that's a different story.'

'I have no fiancé,' Gilda retorted. 'You're the one that had better step softly if you don't want to arouse the jealousy of Comrade Gisella Cibatti.'

Gioli protested, Gilda answered him back, and so they went on for the rest of the journey. Even then the argument wasn't over, and they continued it all the way to Gilda's house. It was dark, and after more discussion Gilda started to say good-bye and go in.

'Too bad,' she said on the threshold, 'that politics should divide us!'

A silly comment, if ever there was one, because a few minutes before, when she and Comrade Gioli had embraced each other, politics hadn't entered into it at all. Love-stories are all exactly the same, and it's absurd that after so many hundreds of thousands of years the human race should take any interest in them. Be that as it may, two evenings later Gilda looked out of her window and saw Gioli sitting on the parapet of the bridge near by. She gazed at him for a while, until sheer annoyance impelled her to go down and ask what he was doing. She was ready for anything and prepared to repay it in kind, but when he said quite simply that he had come in the hope of seeing her, she was so taken aback that he was able to kiss her. Instead of taking offence she decided to reap full advantage from the situation.

'Since this jackass is so crazy about me,' she said to herself, 'I may as well give him some encouragement.

I'll get him to the point where he leaves the Party and then drop him like a hot potato!'

For several evenings Gilda proceeded to encourage him. Then, at the psychological moment, she brought up her heavy artillery.

'Gioli, you swear you love me. Are you willing to prove it?'

'I'm ready for anything.'

'Then get out of that cursed Party! I can't marry a man who's been excommunicated.'

Gioli drew back.

'Gilda, you swear you love me, don't you? Then the burden of the proof is on you. Get out from under those Christian Democrats! I have no intention of marrying a priestess!'

Gilda's tone of voice altered.

'Then you and your filthy Russia can go straight to hell!'

'All right! And while I'm on my merry way, I only hope a fate worse than death overtakes you, and your Vatican and your America!'

Proudly they turned their backs on one another. But the God of lovers had other designs. No sooner had they parted than both their families joined the fray. According to Gioli's relatives and friends, the young man owed it to his own dignity never to look at that pious and pretentious little fraud again. And Gilda's people were equally vociferous in arguing that Gilda ought to give up seeing that dirty Bolshevik for good and all. Both sides hammered away for a whole week, at the end of which time, the mulish Gioli wrote Gilda a special-delivery letter: 'If I look for you tomorrow evening on the bridge in front of your house, will you be there?' To which Gilda made answer: 'I'll meet you at eight o'clock on the Molinetto bridge, where more people will see us!'

They met, then, at eight o'clock, and practically everybody in the village saw them. And those that didn't see them heard about it from those that did. The opposition became more violent than ever. Both Gilda and Gioli found all their friends and acquaintances, including of course their fellow party-members, against them. But the more all these well-intentioned people sought to separate them, the closer they were drawn together.

The subversive Gioli was fundamentally a good boy, and the virtuous Gilda had a strongly rebellious, perhaps even revolutionary nature. Because they were both very proud, they did not speak of the battles they were waging inside their own camps; they relieved their tension by loving each other more and more every day. But when Gilda's people came out with ugly threats, she lost patience.

Peppone was flabbergasted to receive her visit at such a late hour. He wondered what could be the ulterior motive of this girl who had made a fool of one of his most stalwart followers.

'Can you keep a secret until tomorrow morning?' Gilda asked him.

'If it's an honest secret, I can.'

Gilda took out of her pocket-book a card with the party emblem of shield and cross, tore it into pieces, and threw it on to the table.

'Give me one of your cards, now,' she said, 'and keep quiet about it until tomorrow morning. I want to surprise Gioli and also those wretched people who've been trying to get me away from him.'

Peppone remained for several minutes with his mouth hanging open, and then objected:

'But you've come here out of sheer spite. It's not true faith that makes you want to join our party.'

'What does that matter? Since when have you Communists been such sentimental souls that you wouldn't delight in thumbing your noses at the parish priest?'

Peppone had been eating his heart out over the rival

May-Day celebration, and these last words roused a definite reaction.

'I'll make you a member thirty times over, if it will make the priest suffer!'

With card in hand, Gilda went away. And when Peppone had time to think it over, he concluded that Comrade Gioli had scored a personal and party triumph.

'Love is on the Communist side,' he observed sententiously.

The next dawn was that of the First of May and the main square was filled with red, the church square with white carnations. Peppone was overcome by excitement. While on the one hand he hoped to avoid Don Camillo, on the other he would have given almost anything to run into him. Finally they did meet, near the row of low stone columns which separated the two squares.

'Hurrah for Christ the Worker!' exclaimed Peppone, smiling broadly.

'Exactly! He may not have belonged to the union, but He worked as a carpenter, at the side of His father, Joseph.'

'I seem to remember hearing that God was his Father,' Peppone retorted.

'Just so, Mr Mayor. His Father is the greatest Worker of all. He created the universe before there was any such thing as raw materials!'

Peppone swallowed hard and then said between clenched teeth:

'And all the rest of you clerics that are taking part in this labour celebration, just what work do you do?'

'I pray for your sin-stained soul,' said Don Camillo, 'and that's hard work, I can tell you!'

Peppone looked around, and seeing that everything was in good order, he came out with his sensational news:

175

'There's another soul you can pray for,' he said, pointing to a certain segment of the Red throng.

Don Camillo's eyes popped with astonishment. There in a red dress, with a red carnation in her hair, standing close to the red flag, stood Gilda Marossi. What could he say? But before Peppone could enjoy his triumph to the full, a horrible sight met his eye. In the church square, with a white carnation in his buttonhole, practically wrapped in the folds of the Christian-Democrat banner, stood ex-Comrade Angiolino Grisotti. After a moment, Gilda and Gioli caught sight of each other, too, for both of them had been scanning the rival assembly. After standing thunderstruck with amazement they moved instinctively towards the columns dividing the two squares, by which Don Camillo and Peppone still lingered. They exchanged curious glances and then Gilda said:

'I wanted to surprise you!'

'Same here!' said Gioli.

Some of the bystanders burst into laughter. Gilda and Gioli looked into each other's eyes and reached a speechless understanding. As if by preconceived accord they stripped themselves of their carnations, and laid them on one of the low stone columns; then arm in arm they walked away from the centre of the village and out of political life for ever and ever. Don Camillo and Peppone stared raptly at the two carnations.

'Well!...' muttered Peppone, shrugging his shoulders.

'Well! ...' echoed Don Camillo, characteristically throwing out his arms.

And these were the most eloquent speeches that either of them made during this May-Day celebration.